I0452775

BAKER

EVERNIGHT PUBLISHING ®

www.evernightpublishing.com

SAM CRESCENT

BAKER

DEDICATION

I would like to dedicate this to my amazing readers for their patience, their love, and support. Thank you all so much.

BAKER

BAKER

The Skulls, 14

Sam Crescent

Copyright © 2016

Chapter One

One year later from Master

"Everyone is fine at the club. It has been three years since we stopped Gash's brother, Andrew. That guy was sick and twisted. I've never known anything like that before. You'd have hated it, Katie. He hurt a lot of people at the club. Not just The Skulls but Chaos Bleeds. We're healing though. Everyone heals, right?" Baker glanced down at his wedding band, and the pain that had once gripped him, no longer did. Baker, his name, the man he was now. Jaxson Jones, or JJ as many friends had called him, died when he buried his wife and kid. "A lot has happened, a lot has changed. The club doesn't do any more drug runs, and we have a lot of legit businesses in Fort Wills. There's the gym, the bakery, and the mechanic shop."

He stared at the gravestone marking his wife's resting place. "I've changed, Katie. I'm not the same man that got up at three in the morning to bake bread and cookies. I can't keep looking back. There's a woman. A beautiful, charming, loving woman. Her name is Millie Levy, and I've let her down, Katie. We discussed this, didn't we, babe? If either of us died unexpectedly, we had to move on. When we were talking about it, kind of joking around, I never thought I'd actually have to live through it."

He stared up at the sky with dark clouds chasing away the sunlight filled ones.

"I love you, Katie. You and our baby. You'll always be in my heart, and I'll always love you, but it's time for me to move on. I want Millie more than I ever thought possible. I can't just sit and watch her anymore. I need to claim her, and that means it's time for me to go." Removing his ring, Baker pressed a final kiss to the ring, and pulled back a little of the earth. "Rest in peace, baby."

There was no pain, only acceptance, and love.

Taking a deep breath, he turned away from the gravestone to see Fighter standing there waiting. They were both brothers at The Skulls. Fully patched in members.

Fighter had offered to go with him, which Baker was happy about.

"You good?" Fighter asked.

"I'm good."

Baker frowned as Fighter kept looking at him.

"You got a crush on me or something?"

Fighter burst out laughing. "You fucking wish. Nah, I'm good. I just expected tears, or some other girly shit."

Baker shrugged. Five years ago he'd have broken down sobbing for the love that had been taken from him. "Shit happens in life, you know. There's nothing I can do about it." He blew out a breath. "Time to move on, get our shit together."

"Tell me about it. Three years, and we're fucking all alive."

"Kids are growing up. Club is expanding all the time." Baker rubbed the back of his head. One of the reasons he'd prospected for The Skulls was because of how big and bad it was. He'd needed the distraction, to be completely away from everything else he once knew. The only way to do that was to do something completely out of character. He'd always been good at fighting. Strong and big, and always ready for a fight. Of course that anger and aggression had been thrust into baking. Katie had helped him through his anger. With her gone, he'd been lost. The Skulls, Tiny and Lash, they'd helped him to find that focus again.

"I think something is going on with Steven and Sally," Fighter said. They both headed back to their bikes.

Baker frowned. "Nah, she's away at college, and Steven's fucking everything in sight."

"So. Haven't you seen the way he looks at her? It's like she's the only woman in the world."

"Kind of like Simon with Tabitha?" Baker asked, laughing.

Those two kids cracked him up. Simon was the son of Devil, who also happened to be Prez of the Chaos Bleeds crew out in Piston County. Tabitha, she was Tiny's daughter, and Tiny was once Prez of The Skulls until he handed the title over to Lash.

"Please, that boy is going to grow up, and when he realizes he's got to travel to get any action, that will be the end of that romance," Fighter said.

"I doubt it. Once you find that woman, you'll do anything. Even travel miles to get a kiss."

"Speaking of special women, you heard the news about Millie?"

Baker tensed up. "What news?"

"She's got a date."

"Who the fuck with?" Baker had not heard of any date. Millie never went out with anyone. She kept to herself, and only visited the club when she was invited.

"Some doctor who works at the hospital with Sandy. They were having dinner, and the next thing you know, he's asking her out on a date."

"Doctor? Sandy works with old guys."

"Not Doctor Banks. He transferred to Fort Wills, and guess what, he's got an eye out for your girl. Wait, can we really call her your girl? She dumped your ass."

"We were never going out."

"Oh, that's right. You fucked it up."

"I thought you were here to be supportive?"

"I am being supportive. I'm telling you how big of an ass you've been letting Millie get away."

"I didn't let her get away."

"You didn't claim her ass, did you?"

Baker glared. "Fuck you."

Fighter burst out laughing. "I think you did what you wanted to do."

"What's that?"

"Closure. You're ready to move on."

Baker didn't argue. He couldn't. This was either going to make or break him. Before leaving to go to the graveyard where his wife and baby rested, he'd made himself a promise. If he couldn't handle saying goodbye one final time, he wouldn't leave. He'd hand in his patch, and cut Fort Wills out of his life.

The pull of Millie was too great. He couldn't be without her anymore. There was a time when he'd felt guilty for the feelings she inspired. No more.

He wanted her all to himself. Now he just had to find a way to prove it to her. If a fucking doctor was sniffing after her, he had to find a way to prove to Millie he was ready.

She was right. She deserved a man who'd love her for her. Not some guy who was still mourning his dead wife.

"Time to go home," Baker said. Time to get back to Fort Wills, and to win over the woman that had belonged to him.

****

"I didn't know if you'd like Italian or not. I've not been in Fort Wills long, and I wanted to impress you."

"It's fine," Millie said, smiling across the table at her date. It was nice being asked on a date, something out of the ordinary for her. Being a toy shop owner, she wasn't exactly popular. Guys tried to avoid her because of the whole toy shop persona, and especially with her being a woman. It was like they assumed she wanted kids, lots of them. "I was surprised you asked me out, Doctor Banks."

"Please, call me Jack."

"Jack."

"I'm Doctor Banks every other day. Tonight I just want to be Jack, and you Millie."

"I can appreciate that. Did you always want to be a doctor?"

"I come from a family of them. I'm an only child. Both of my parents are doctors, and of course my grandparents are as well."

"So you had a lot of responsibility to follow in their footsteps?"

"More like curiosity. At the dinner table they were always talking about a surgery, or a disease, or something. I was a curious kid, and I wanted to know everything. It didn't take me long to find the medical journals, and I was hooked. Anyway, enough about me. What about you? Sandy told me you own the toy shop."

"Yes. If you want modern or vintage toys, I'm your gal."

"Are you an only child?"

"Erm, no, I'm actually the youngest. I have a sister."

"What's she doing?"

Millie stared down at the table. "I don't know. I've not been back home in over nine years, and I have no intention of going back."

Jack held his hands up. "I asked too much?"

"No, of course not. I just, there's nothing to say. Why did you come to Fort Wills?" she asked, avoiding the subject.

"Why not? It's a nice little town, and I love it here. Of course the resident MC intrigued me."

"The Skulls?"

"Yeah, I'd heard about them. They had a lot of reputation. I also know that Sandy is married to one."

"Stink. I like the club. They're good guys."

"They're a bunch of criminals, right?"

She shook her head. "No. They're not. Everything I've seen, they're good guys. They've just had some hard times." Millie wasn't overly close with any of The Skulls. She loved the old ladies that came into her shop, but they weren't really close. Millie had never been able to get close to anyone.

"I've touched a nerve again."

"I know they've lost a lot, and I don't believe you should be judging them. You don't know them." She looked around the restaurant, suddenly wishing for the date to end.

"I'm so sorry. I know Sandy is one of them. I really shouldn't have said anything."

"You really shouldn't. I'm a believer in not judging a book by its cover. The Skulls are a book."

"You're very passionate about that."

She thought about Baker. He wasn't a bad person, and even though there was never going to be anything between them, she didn't want anyone bad-mouthing him.

"I am." She was just about to put an end to their date when her name was called.

"Millie, it's great to see you."

She turned to see Angel approaching.

Feeling saved a little, Millie smiled and stood. "Angel, how are you?"

"I'm doing good. It's date night, and I've been asking Lash to bring me here for ages. I wanted to find out if the food is as good as Eva's been bragging about. Have you tried it?"

"We have yet to order. This is my, erm, date, Jack."

"You're the doctor," Lash said, finally drawing attention to himself.

Millie was surprised to see Lash dressed in a business suit.

"I'm the doctor. Your name is Lash?"

"I'm the Prez of The Skulls. Sandy's told me all about you."

Turning to Angel, Millie forced a smile.

"I've been meaning to talk to you for the past few days," Angel said.

"I've been at the shop."

"Anthony has been a little bit of a handful, and Chloe's walking around now, and she's into everything."

"I think it's time for us to order," Jack said, interrupting them.

Millie cringed. "We'll talk soon."

13

Giving Angel a quick hug, she sat back down, and waited for whatever Jack was about to say. He nodded at the waiter, and Millie started to get uncomfortable. He was really rude, which was a shock. Shouldn't doctors be nice and patient?

"I guess a life of crime pays," Jack said, muttering.

Staring at her menu, and then across the table, she just couldn't do it. She'd accepted the dinner invite because she imagined it would have been fun. This was not fun. This was far from fun.

"You know what, this was a mistake." She closed the menu. Opening her purse, she left enough for the water, and the service she'd received. "I don't see a point in either of us continuing this date. I'm sorry." She got to her feet and left the table. Even when he called her name, she didn't stop. Millie had made a vow to never be in uncomfortable situations, or to prolong something that was not going anywhere. She liked The Skulls. Fort Wills had thrived in recent years. Sure, there had been some hardships and death, but that was all in the past. Jack hadn't even met the club, and he was judging them.

She was walking out of the restaurant, and turned a corner when she hit a large, firm, male chest.

"Oh, I'm so sorry," she said, looking up to see that she'd just walked into Baker.

"You don't need to apologize," he said, holding onto her arms to steady her.

"I should have watched where I was going."

"You were moving quite fast. I'm fine though. I like having you in my arms." She stared at his arms, and couldn't help but feel protected. Baker had done everything he could to protect her when the club had been under threat. He could have left her. He didn't. "Do you mind me asking what you were running from?"

"A judgy date. What about you?"

"I'm heading in to speak to Lash."

"Oh, well he's just sat down to the—"

"That's a lie."

"Oh, it is?"

"Yeah, I wasn't going to see Lash. Couldn't give a shit about crashing his date."

"Then why are you here?"

She stared at him, waiting, wondering.

"Millie," Jack said, calling from behind her.

She couldn't help but cringe as she felt her date coming toward them.

Crap, crap, crap.

Staring up at Baker, she saw he'd already clocked Jack.

Turning around, she stared at Jack as he came toward her. "You didn't need to leave."

"Actually, I did. This is not going to go anywhere, and we don't see eye to eye, even on a first date."

"Who is this?" Jack asked, looking at Baker.

"I'm Baker." His hand came over her shoulder, and she saw the ring of his dragon tattoo around her wrist as his jacket pulled back a little.

"Hello," Jack said.

She watched as the two men shook hands, and Baker squeezed his hand. She saw the whiteness of Baker's knuckles. Jack looked in pain, and she winced, putting her hand over theirs. "That's okay."

Separating their hands, she released them, and stepped away.

"She doesn't want to date you," Baker said.

"We're different people, Jack."

"So you're cutting this date short?"

"Yes."

15

Jack stared at Baker's patch. "Now I understand why you were sticking up for them."

She tensed up, but didn't say anything else.

"Oh well, it's not a waste. You're not really my type." Jack walked away, and Millie wasn't surprised. He wasn't the first man to insult her, and he certainly wouldn't be the last.

"Ignore that asshole," Baker said.

"Don't worry about it. I'm going to head home."

"I came to the restaurant tonight because I heard about your date. I was going to crash it."

She laughed. "You should know he hates the MC. I'd advise all the people at the club not to even bother visiting him, or using him at the hospital. He hates The Skulls, and he's not even known you guys."

"Sounds like a total asshole to me."

"He is." Tucking some of her curls behind her ear, she found that she didn't actually want to leave. "I better head home."

"I can take you. Let me walk with you so I'm not tempted to go and ruin Lash and Angel's date. It has been too long since the two of them have gotten anything done. I'd be the devil."

"Sure. I'd like the company."

He offered his arm, and she placed her arm through his, holding onto him. "So if he didn't want to date you, why the hell did he invite you out for dinner?" he asked.

"I don't know. I think he's a bit of an asshole. He went on the defense. The moment he saw Lash and Angel, he was just saying some really horrible nasty stuff, and I couldn't handle it. You once told me that I didn't have to force myself to do something I didn't want to do. I decided I didn't want to be on a date with someone who was saying nasty stuff about my friends."

"You finally see us as your friends?"

"That's what you are, right?"

"Baby, we are. You don't have to doubt it. Angel is always a little upset that she has to see you to invite you over. You never come over."

"Oh, erm, I really don't want to impose, or for you guys to think that I'm invading your space."

"The clubhouse is huge, and we have a lot of people over. Not to mention the club whores. Their numbers are dwindling though. The Skulls is no longer a conventional club."

"Conventional?"

"Club whores, drugs runs, that kind of stuff."

"Wow, you really were a bad boy."

"Exactly, I *was* a bad boy. I'm not anymore."

She squeezed his arm, loving his company. "It's getting cold."

"Yes. Millie, I didn't like you being on a date." She didn't say anything. What more was there to say? "I was coming to stop it. I don't want you to date anyone else."

"Anyone else?"

"We've danced around this for a few years, and I want us to date."

"Baker?"

"Hear me out." He stopped and grabbed her hands. "I'm ready. I know what you wanted me to wait for, and I've done it." He held up his hand, and she was shocked to see his wedding band was gone.

"What did you do?"

"It's time for me to move on, right? I'm ready. I can't lose you, and I won't do it."

Millie's heart was pounding. "Baker?"

"There's no reason for us to not to be together. I'm here. I'm ready." He released her hand, and cupped her cheek. "I want you."

Licking her lips, she saw the need in his eyes, and knew without a doubt that he was speaking the truth.

What was wrong with giving in?

The ring he always wore was gone, and she couldn't help but notice that his gaze wasn't filled with pain. Even when he came to the shop, she always saw the love and pain for his wife.

"How about we agree to go on a date?" she asked.

"Not the Italian place. I don't want you to think of that asshole when you're dating with me."

"How about I leave you to pick the place? I like everything."

"Baby, that is a challenge. It'll be perfect."

"I don't need perfect, Baker. I never did." Then, going against everything, she pressed her lips to his. It wasn't anything special. She simply pressed her lips against his. The pleasure she got from that small touch completely shocked her. Breaking away, she saw his eyes had closed, and the look of bliss on his face made her toes curl.

"I'm going to remember this moment for the rest of my life," he said.

"You know how to charm." They stopped outside of her shop. "This is me."

Baker cupped her cheek, and pressed a kiss to her lips. "I'll call you tomorrow night."

Without saying another word, Millie made her way into her home, and couldn't wait until the next day.

Chapter Two

The following day Baker made his way downstairs at seven o'clock. What he found in the kitchen was chaos. Angel was rushing around, shoving sandwiches into lunchboxes as Eva was feeding the babies. Everywhere he turned, one woman was rushing around.

"What happened?" he asked.

"They've got a trip today," Lacey said, pouring water into the goblets.

"We thought it'd be good if we all stayed at the clubhouse today," Tate said. "That way we could get them to school."

"We've got to leave in ten minutes," Angel said, starting the countdown.

"I'm pleased I don't have any kids," Fighter said. "This is just too crazy."

"Shut up!" Tate glared at the brother, and began to rush around once again preparing everything that needed to be done for the school trip.

Baker walked in, and made his way around the kitchen, trying not to bump into anyone. The last thing he wanted to worry about was being the person who ruined the kids' school trip.

"So, erm, where are they going?" he asked, pouring some coffee into his cup.

"We're going to the zoo," Tabitha said. "Simon told me all about the zoo. It's awesome."

They all knew she wasn't talking about Tate's son, Simon. No, Tabitha was talking about Devil's son, Simon. The Prez of the Chaos Bleeds.

"You'll get to see it now, won't you, honey?" Eva said.

"Yeah. Dad is so tired of hearing about Simon though. He says that he's got a son, and he's more interested in him. He's got two sons." Tabitha shrugged. "I don't care. I love Simon. We're going to get married."

Baker laughed, and quickly turned it into a cough. Tabitha was adorable. The two kids were adorable, but in recent months they'd not seen much of the Chaos Bleeds crew. They'd either come for Thanksgiving, Christmas, or a special barbeque.

"It's fine. It's fine," Angel said. "Ha, eight lunchboxes for eight kids on the trip. Plus the rest for the kids going to nursery." She pushed some of her blonde hair that had fallen. "I totally rock."

Out of all of the women, Angel was the sweetest he'd ever known. Of course, Millie was fast taking over in that regard. Both women were so damn sweet, and it just annoyed the hell out of him the thought of anyone doing something awful to them.

"Are we ready?" Lash asked, walking into the clubhouse, sipping on his coffee.

All the kids shouted yes, causing them all to laugh.

"Oh, just a warning, Sally's on her way home today with Drew," Lacey said, grabbing empty bowls.

"She is?" Steven asked, walking into the room.

"Yeah. She doesn't want to be at the campus this weekend, and Drew needed to come home for some kind of family dinner. I don't know the whole reasons, but there you go. Whizz offered to pick her up, but seeing as Drew was already coming home, she turned it down." Lacey shrugged.

"Yay, Sally's coming home," Daisy said, throwing her arms up. The young girl had moved so suddenly that she tripped back.

Before any of them could stop her, she started to

fall back, about to have her head hit the floor.

Anthony was there, grabbing her and tugging her up.

"Wow!" Daisy said. "That could have been horrible."

"Sweetie, what have I told you about that?" Lacey said, hands on her hips. "You keep falling over just lately. We're going to need to get you a crash helmet."

Daisy scrunched up her nose.

"That's okay. I'm here to stop her falling," Anthony said.

"That's my boy." This came from Lash. "We're ready to move out."

One by one, the kids grabbed their lunchboxes, and Baker watched as all of the kids, old ladies, and dads left. The once chaotic kitchen had changed, becoming silent and calm.

"Now that sound is bizarre as fuck," Fighter said.

"You missing them already?" Baker asked.

"Yeah. When it's noisy I think of the peace and quiet I'm going to get. Now I just want them back. Damn, I love kids."

He chuckled. "Yeah, you're totally not going to have kids."

Fighter gave him the finger.

Steven interrupted them by dragging out a chair, and slumping down.

"Shouldn't you be in a good fucking mood?" Fighter asked.

"What the fuck for?"

"Duh, your girl is heading home."

Baker rolled his eyes.

"Sally is not my girl."

"Could have fooled me. The way you are with

her, there's no way she's *not* yours," Fighter said.

"You know she's of age now. You don't have to worry about breaking the law."

"Ugh, that's the least of my worries." Steven rubbed at his eyes. "Sally's not mine."

Sally was Whizz and Lacey's adoptive daughter. She'd been through so much shit that she was years older than her actual age, which was twenty-one. She would be twenty-one in a couple of months. Nearly four years ago the club had been attacked by a guy who was looking for revenge. Andrew, Gash's brother, had paid a gang to do a drive by shooting. In the process it had shot through Sally's knee. The doctors had been unable to save her leg from the knee down, and now she had a prosthetic.

Baker would never forget how much it had changed the young girl. She'd become even more withdrawn and quiet.

"So you're going to let her little jock take her from you?" Baker asked.

"She's not mine. If I wanted the third fucking degree I'd have gone with the women. Stop being a pussy."

Baker shrugged. "You're in a shit mood this morning."

"Of course he was. Last night he was on the booze. For someone who doesn't care about the little woman, he sure drowns his sorrows like he does."

Steven got up and left the kitchen. Baker no longer thought it was funny. He knew what Steven was going through. When the shit ended with Andrew four years back, Millie had walked away from him. Now, he had a chance to win her back, and he wasn't going to let anything get in this way.

Finishing off his coffee, he got to work on putting the mess to rights. The club pussy was down to only a few girls. Most of the old ladies took care of the work. Baker smiled thinking about how much the club had changed since he'd been a member. In three years they hadn't had a single attack, and for that he was grateful.

When it came to the love of the club, he couldn't handle the thought of any of them in pain.

"You don't have to do that," Angel said, coming into the kitchen. She wasn't carrying her daughter, so she must have dropped her off at the nursery.

"I don't mind. You do enough."

"I made this mess. The least I can do is clean it up."

"You're always taking care of the club." He didn't stop drying the dishes that he'd just finished. Angel started on the rest of the table. Baker was going to do it in stages, but Angel lined all of the dishes up next to the washing bowl.

"I like taking care of people. Lash has his place within the club, and I want to be part of that, I want to be part of him."

Out of everyone at the club, Lash and Angel had one of those special kinds of relationships. They gravitated to each other, and they were always touching or whispering. Nothing could come between them. Baker had seen firsthand the way that Lash had gone crazy when something happened to Angel.

"You are."

"He's doing a hell of a good job right now, don't you think?" She sounded so proud. "He is. I think even Tiny's impressed. At least I hope he is. It's been a bit of a nervous time. Crap, I don't know if I should be talking."

Baker laughed. "Don't worry, Angel. We're all family here."

"Speaking of family, did you know Millie just

walked out on her date last night? It surprised me."

"I know. I also know he was talking shit about the club. She had our backs."

"That evil … man."

"You can swear you know. Last time I checked you were allowed."

"I know it's just wrong. I don't like to bring that to the club. There's always a better way to say stuff, and I'm determined to make sure all of our kids know it."

"They're probably cussing better than us."

She smiled. "Not in front of me, and certainly not in front of their teachers."

"Did I tell you that I've got a date?"

"You have? Who with?"

"Millie."

She turned to him and let out a squeal. "You finally got her to agree to go on a date."

"Yep."

"Oh wow, this is such good news."

"I thought so."

"I'd give you a big hug right now, but because I'm covered in water, I can't."

"Hey, no hugging my wife," Lash said, coming into the kitchen. "Good luck on your date. Don't screw it up."

"Lash!"

"I won't. I've learned from my mistake."

"I noticed you dropped the wedding band. Does that mean you're ready?"

"Lash, have you ever heard of a filter?" Angel asked.

"This guy has spent the past few years panting after that woman like a little puppy dog. Forgive me for wanting to make sure he's not going to come crying to us when it doesn't work out."

Baker burst out laughing. "It's true. I've been particularly miserable because *I* fucked up."

"See, even he agrees with me."

"I'll never ever understand you. Never," Angel said.

Lash walked up behind her, wrapping his arms around her. "Good, I still need to be mysterious to make you want me."

"You don't have to be anything to make me want you."

And that was Baker's cue to leave.

****

Millie finished putting the latest batch of teddy bears onto the shelves, and she checked each one to make sure there was no fault. The last thing she wanted was for the bears to be faulty, for a kid to fall in love with them, and her have to take it back because the stuffing was coming out. Millie loved teddy bears. Even though she was twenty-nine years old, she still had her favorite one on her bed. When she was ever upset or ill, she would hold that bear with a death grip.

"There we go," she said. "All perfect."

Taking the box out into the back, she then threw the small boxes inside, and carried it toward the back door. She'd take everything out at the end of the day. Millie was making her way into the main shop when the doorbell rang letting her know someone had entered her shop.

"You're going on a date with Baker?" Angel asked, entering the shop.

She smiled. "Yeah, he asked me on one last night."

"He just told me about it. I was helping clean the kitchen from the mess I trashed, and he just blurted it out. Are you excited?" Angel asked.

"A little. I'm nervous as well. It's my first date in like ever. Last night didn't count. I didn't even get to eat. This will be the first one with Baker."

"Didn't you go to dinner with Hardy and Rose?"

"Yeah, I did but at the time I didn't really think that was a date." Baker had been there, and she'd thought it was just a friendly meal that he'd been invited to. She'd never known he'd wanted anything to do with her. When he'd tried to make it clear that he wanted her, he'd still been wearing a wedding band. There was no way she was ever going to give herself to a man who still loved his wife. For once in her life she was determined to come first place, no matter what.

"Did you even know he was into you?"

"Not really, no. I thought he was a nice guy who had a really big love for kids' stuff." Baker had been stopping by the shop for months prior to her dinner with Hardy and Rose. He always bought little trinkets for the kids, or was always there for the big deliveries when The Skulls decided to order.

"I think it's great what is happening to you two," Angel said. "I keep telling you to come by the club, but you won't listen."

"I don't want to intrude."

"You won't be. I happen to enjoy your company, and would love for you to come around the club more often." Angel moved toward her and hugged her.

Millie smiled, and gave her a little squeeze. "It's just never really been my place. I'm not being mean or anything. I don't want you to think I'm ungrateful to The Skulls."

"I know you're not, sweetie. We're your friends. All of us, and we care about you."

"You're one of the sweetest women I know."

"Lash says I am all the time. I just think there is

enough evil in the world that I don't want to add to it. I'm hoping everyone finds a smile with me."

Millie moved away, and rounded the counter to grab what she figured Angel was here for.

"I didn't come to pick up my order. I came to plan for your date. You need my help?"

"I don't know what we're doing, so I doubt it. It's Baker, so I'm just going to dress normally."

"You looked hot last night," Angel said.

"You think so?"

"Yeah, Baker told me that the guy was judging The Skulls."

"He was. I'd say he was a total a-hole." Millie shook her head. "I don't even know if Sandy knew how bad he was."

"I doubt it. They work together, but from what I hear, Sandy doesn't exactly talk about the club. It's her personal and private business." Angel flicked some of her hair off her shoulder, and jumped as the door was thrust open.

"You're on a date with Baker?" Lacey asked, coming in. She carried a large bag that Millie had noticed she carried around a lot.

The Skulls had taken over the spa in town, and along with it, there was now a beauty shop that Lacey part owned.

"Wow, news really does travel fast."

"It's The Skulls, baby, we all know people's business. Also, you've got to realize that we're our own little community. Plus, Baker's telling everyone. I heard it from him. He's so damn happy that you've finally caved to him."

Millie laughed. "Really?"

"Yeah, I've never seen him so damn happy," Lacey said, dropping her case onto the counter. "So I've come to help. I'm thinking we can color your hair. Such a beautiful color, but I want to enhance that look."

All of a sudden Lacey had her hands on Millie's hair and was running her fingers through it.

"You certainly look after your hair. This is beautiful."

"Thank you, I think."

"I've dealt with women with split ends, dry as fuck, and they just don't deserve hair." Lacey gave a shiver. "Now I can work with this."

"I really don't think it's necessary."

"Babe, we love you, we really do, but I've never seen Baker so damn happy. This has to work because I don't want to see his miserable ass around the club."

Lacey was the complete opposite of Angel. Both women were nice, but just had different ways of showing it.

Millie took a deep breath. "It's lunchtime."

"I know, so we've got plenty of time to get you ready."

Her shop door opened again, and she was shocked to see Rose, Kelsey, Tate, Prue, and Eva enter her store.

"We're the ones that have come to help," Eva said.

"The others had to work, or are on children duty," Tate said.

"Wow, all of this is so I keep Baker happy?" Millie asked.

"It's completely selfish of us," Prue said, jumping up onto the counter. "Baker is like this sucking the life right out of you look to him. I don't want to see him like that anymore. So we're hoping to give you all the good points that make him so awesome."

"I adore him," Kelsey said. "He's great with kids,

and I want to see him happy."

Before long the shop was closed, and Millie was urged into her home, which was above her shop. She loved being able to get up and go to work. Also, she loved working for herself.

Within seconds, music was on, and Lacey had all of her stuff out on the kitchen counters.

"Who is picking up the kids?" Lacey asked.

"Whizz and Lash," Angel said.

"Did you know Charlotte and Gash have gone away again?" Tate asked.

Several of the women nodded their heads. Charlotte and Gash were expecting a little baby, and Millie helped them a few weeks ago to pick out some baby toys. She'd never seen a woman so nervous about having a baby. Charlotte was constantly rubbing her stomach, and looking worried that her baby was going to disappear.

"They deserve to go out and travel. When their daughter is here, they won't have so much time, and they'll be wishing they took it," Prue said.

"Regretting kids?" Tate asked.

"Fuck off, Tate. No, I'm not regretting having kids. I think we need some of our time. You know, girls' time. It has been too long since we just had some fun."

"Yeah, try three years since we had some fun," Eva said.

"Since Andrew," Lacey said. "If I could go back in time, I would so like to gut that man! Every time I see Sally hurting, and she does, even with her prosthetic." Lacey shook her head. "I know it still pisses Whizz off. We promise to protect her, and what happens? She gets shot and loses her leg. I'm a fucking awful mother."

They all booed and disagreed.

"Sweetie, you're a fantastic mother, and Sally

adores you," Angel said.

"I'm with Angel. You're a wonderful mother, and I don't think you should do shit like that. None of us could stop what Andrew was going to do." Tate hugged Lacey close. "We all promised each other that we wouldn't talk about this."

"I tried to save Happy. He took a bullet for me, and I wanted to save him," Millie said. Many nights after the drive by shooting, she'd been so damn scared. She'd dreamt of Happy for so long.

"Again, it's no one's fault. It's Andrew's and Russell's. Both men are dead," Prue said.

They all shared a look, and Millie felt one with each of them. They had all been hurt by Andrew and his partner in evil.

After a few moments, Lacey pushed Millie down into a chair. "Let's make you so beautiful that Baker is kicking himself for waiting so long."

Chapter Three

Baker knocked on Millie's door and waited. Several of The Skull women had disappeared, and he knew without a doubt they were helping his woman get ready. There was no way that any of the men would allow their women out of sight or for so long if they didn't know where they were.

The door opened, and he saw Angel smiling. "Hey, Baker."

"Is Millie ready?" he asked.

"She is."

One by one the missing Skull women left the house, and there right at the end was Millie. She was dressed in a pair of jeans that fit her beautiful curves, and a red shirt that seemed to thrust her tits out.

"Wow," he said.

Then he noticed her hair had been dyed, purple underneath with black hair on top. It was curled to make the colors pop out. She was the most beautiful woman he'd ever seen. From the moment he first saw her, he'd thought that.

"Hey," he said, finding his voice a little husky.

"Hey yourself."

Lacey nudged him in the side. "You're very welcome. Come on, girls, we've been gone long enough."

Within minutes they were alone.

"I like them," she said.

"They clearly like you." He didn't doubt that they liked her.

"I had no idea where we were going, or what we're doing. If you need me to go and change—"

"You're perfect, Millie. Can I confess

something?"

"Sure."

"I don't have a clue what to do tonight. I just want you all to myself, and without the club, or pressures. Just you and me."

Millie smiled. "Then let's go and make this a date together."

He squeezed her hand, and she paused when she saw his bike.

"Please, for me, give it a try."

"Bikes are kind of scary."

"You'll have a reason to hold onto me." He couldn't resist grabbing her hips. They were so full, and he wanted her. His cock thickened, and he pressed his lips against her neck, breathing in her scent.

She drove him fucking crazy, and she didn't even know what the hell she was doing to him. It was like a spell that only Millie could weave.

"Baker?"

"Yeah, I'm hungry."

"Shit, sorry." Grabbing the helmet, he held it out to her.

"Not a chance. Do you know how much Lacey pulled, tugged, and tweezed to get this hair like this? I'm scared to move in case my hair literally falls off my head."

He burst out laughing. "It makes me wonder at times how she is so busy."

"The woman is a sadist."

Baker didn't like the thought of her going without a helmet, but he wasn't about to force the issue. He'd drive carefully, and he was confident with his skills. They would both be safe.

Straddling his bike, he waited for her to get on comfortably. He noticed she didn't grab him too hard, and he rolled his eyes.

"You've got to hold right on tight to me, babe." Taking hold of her hands, he wrapped them around his waist, and she snuggled in close.

"Take me to get some food, Baker."

Then she kissed his neck.

Starting up the engine, he pulled away from her shop, and headed out of town toward a bar that served food, sometimes had a band, and a dance-floor, Ronald's bar. It wasn't luxurious, but it was good. He'd never seen a fight break out, and it took them away from the prying eyes of The Skulls.

He felt as she leaned back a little, looking up at the sky.

"Whoop, this is great!" She screamed the words, and he loved seeing her let go.

Millie held onto him tightly still, her jean covered cunt calling to him as it pressed against his back. He wanted more than anything to stop somewhere, and fuck her. This was how it always felt around her. She filled him with so much need that it was hard for him to think of anything else.

She wrapped her arms around him, hugging him tight for several seconds before loosening her hold and enjoying the rush of wind over her face.

By the time he pulled up outside of Ronald's bar, Millie looked full of life and passion. Her eyes sparkled, and even though she fell on her ass getting off his bike, Baker found it an enjoyable excuse to put his hands back on her. Several cars and bikes were parked outside.

"Are you allowed to be here? Isn't there some law about bikers or something?"

"There's no other MC here, and I'm not in anyone else's territory. I wouldn't do that to you."

"Okay. I don't want you to get into trouble for

just taking me out."

"That would never happen, I promise."

Unable to resist, he dropped a kiss to her lips. "Now, let's go and get you food."

Once inside the bar, he found a table that offered them a little privacy but allowed them to see everything going on inside the bar. Years of The Skulls finding trouble had made it impossible for him to actually relax.

"I like it here," she said. "It has a really good vibe. Have you been here before?"

"A couple of times. Just because I wanted to be alone and stare at the beer bottle, or wonder what the fuck I'm doing. I came here a lot after you left."

"I didn't really leave. I just went home."

"You left, and I knew it was all my fault."

"It wasn't."

He reached out, taking her hand. Running his thumb across her knuckles, he stared into her eyes at the same time. "It was my fault. Everything you said to me wasn't wrong. I loved my wife, and I'm not going to lie to you. I still love my wife. I will always love her, and I doubt that will ever change. She holds a place in my heart. The only difference is the fact that it's not the same. She's there, but she's not. Does that make sense?"

"I think so. You don't have to not talk about her, you know."

"I don't want to hurt you."

"You won't. We all have a past. I accept that. How did you meet her?"

"Katie was my high school sweetheart. I fell in love with her when we were kids. Obviously I didn't have a clue what it meant until later. The moment I did, I knew I was going to marry her, have kids."

"How do you know you're ready to move on?" she asked.

He held his hand up, showing his empty ring finger. "Memories are all well and good, but they don't keep you warm at night. I haven't been warm in a long time, Millie. I want to have a life, and not just look back wishing for another woman. I want you."

She licked her lips. "Wow, you really know how to make a girl feel special."

"Do you believe me?" he asked.

"Yeah, I do." She opened her mouth and then closed it. "We all have a past, and I have, had, a fiancé."

"What?"

"Yes. Ten plus years ago. I was nineteen, and young, and stupid. The guy I had been dating in high school asked me to marry him, and I was so convinced that I loved him, I said yes. We hadn't had sex or anything." He saw her cheeks had gone a really deep shade of red. She didn't stop talking though. "I should have known it wasn't meant to be. I mean, he'd never even tried to be with me, you know."

"Have sex with you?"

"You know how most girls are supposed to be pressured or whatever? I never was. He was this sweet guy, and I thought he was what I wanted."

"What happened?"

She stared down at his hands. "He was having sex with a girl I know. I walked in on my wedding day as they were fucking. They didn't know I could see them, or that I was there, and I heard them talking. Sucked."

"I had no idea."

"I'm going to go a little personal right now and say that all my life I have always been second best. No one has ever wanted me for me, or they've always wanted me to do something, or it was because I was there, and their other friend wasn't. When I came to Fort Wills, I promised myself that I wouldn't be second best anymore. I wouldn't settle for second best."

He gave her hand a squeeze, amazed as she batted away her tears. Baker wondered if she'd learned to do that a lot.

"You'll never be second best to me."

"I don't mind waiting."

"There's something I'm curious about," he said, staying on topic but changing it a little.

"Yeah."

"You said you didn't have sex with your guy, and then you moved to Fort Wills. Have you ever had sex?"

Her mouth opened wide, and then closed.

"You're a virgin?"

"You know it's really rude to do what you're doing," she said, looking around the bar.

"No one can hear us, and if they could, they really wouldn't care. You're a virgin?"

"Yeah, I'm a virgin. I'd appreciate it if you didn't go and announce it to the entire world."

Baker nodded. "Well, I didn't expect that."

She glared at him, and picked up the menu.

"I'm not a virgin."

"I already know that."

"I can teach you a thing or two. I have this trick with my tongue—"

"Baker, this is supposed to be a date."

"I'm not judging you. I'm advertising my skills. Haven't you ever been curious about it?"

"Sure, I have. I've just never wanted to do something like that with someone I didn't know. It hasn't been exactly hard to stay this way, Baker. There's not thousands of hot men, or ugly men, banging down my door to go on a date."

"All it takes is one."

"Yeah, so?"

"I'm right here, Millie, and I'd gladly break your door down to get to you."

Her mouth had opened slightly, and he saw that her nipples poked against the front of her shirt. She was curious, and he was going to work with that.

"If you ever feel the need to experiment, or find out what you like, I'm your guy."

"Baker, are you being serious?"

"Deadly serious."

"Wow, you're full of surprises today."

"The night is young."

****

"Am I better than Millie?"

"Fuck, baby, even if I let Millie get close, you're the best. I'm going to have to put a bag over her head to fuck her."

Millie would never forget the horrible words she'd heard. She'd truly believed that Brian had been a sweet man when in fact, he'd found it easier to hide who he really was. Five years they were dating, and in all of that time, she never once suspected that he'd been cheating on her, or that he despised her.

After finding him screwing *her* on the day she was due to get married, Millie couldn't take it. She'd gone back to her room where everyone else at the wedding was more interested in their own stuff, and she'd simply left her own wedding. No one had stopped her, even as she climbed into a car in her wedding dress. It had been like she didn't exist in this world, or that no one even cared that she was running away from the guy she was supposed to marry.

Once she got home, she'd packed her bag and left. The wedding dress was wrapped up in a bag in her attic. She hadn't been able to bring herself to throw it out. The dress had cost a fortune, and had meant so much to her at the time.

She had been second best her entire life.

The moment she entered Fort Wills, she'd felt at home, and known without a doubt that this was where she was going to stay.

"The night is young, huh?" she asked.

"Neither of us has to be back by a curfew. How do you feel to spending some time with this badass biker?"

She giggled. "Badass?"

"I am bad."

"You bake, Baker. I wouldn't exactly call that a bad profession. It's … sweet."

"I'm a sweet guy as well as bad."

"All right then, bad boy. What's good here?" she asked.

Baker went and ordered their food after they had decided what they wanted. They both were having the steak with fries, onion rings, and the works. Her mouth watered just thinking about the food. He came back with some drinks. She was surprised to see he had the same as hers.

Millie didn't drink, and he'd remembered that.

"So, are you going to give me a chance? You can test drive me if you like?"

Sipping her drink, she rolled her eyes. "You're not going to stop, are you?"

"I can, but the question is, do you want to?"

It was nice to have a guy hitting on her. "No, I don't want you to stop. So, tell me about you, Baker? Something knew that I've never heard before."

"There's not much to tell. You know I was married, and I had a baby on the way. I was a baker, and I sold up shop to move out here. Being a prospect wasn't exactly my plan. I liked The Skulls, and I knew it was where I needed to be. Now I'm a patched in member, I'm happy."

"I never thought I'd be a toy shop owner. I love it, and don't get me wrong it's amazing, but I thought I'd be a wife and mother. It's interesting how everything changes, don't you think?"

"It's life, baby. We're always being challenged, and having shit thrown our way, and that way." He took hold of her hands once again. "Do you wish you weren't in Fort Wills?"

"No. This is my home."

"You don't miss your family?"

She thought about her family, and their complete lack of love for her. Even with her being in Fort Wills, no one had come to visit her. They probably found her embarrassing. Her family was wealthy. Not newsworthy of course, but the kind that came from old money.

Biting her lip, she didn't know how to answer without making herself sound terrible. "No, I don't." She averted her gaze, hating how much she actually disliked her family.

"They must have really done a number on you to feel like that."

She looked at him. "You don't think I'm mean or nasty?"

"No. I think you've clearly been hurt enough that you don't want to revisit them." He didn't say anything more.

"Thank you for not prying."

"You'll tell me the truth when you're ready."

Their food came out, and she stared at the steak, her mouth watering.

"This looks so good." Grabbing a fry, she took a bite and moaned. Sometimes fried comfort food was exactly the best thing in the world.

Eating food with Baker turned out to be a lot of fun. He didn't stare at her every time she took a bite of steak or ate a fry. He even dipped one of his in the spicy dipping sauce he ordered, to give her a try. It was nice not to be judged, and she used to be. Brian would spend a lot of time telling her what she should and shouldn't do.

"Normal women diet, Millie."

"You should really watch your waistline. It's getting bigger."

"Do you know how fat you're getting?"

The insults had kept on coming, and she'd hated it. She'd spend most of their dates pushing food around her plate.

"Damn, I love a woman who knows how to eat," Baker said, sitting back.

She'd already stopped eating because she was full, and she was on a new diet. Tonight was going to be difficult to work off, but she was determined to lose at least two dress sizes, or three. She was a size eighteen, and she wanted to be either a twelve, or try for a ten.

Baker finished his plate, and hers, until there was nothing left.

"You must think I'm a pig," he said.

"Not at all. You're a big guy. You need to keep a lot of food to keep you going."

"Food is a good way of keeping my energy up."

She saw the wicked glint in his eye. "You're not even talking about food, are you?"

"I am, just what good it can do."

"Sex?"

"That's one of them."

"You're not going to stop?"

"I *can* stop, but you see, Millie, I'm not going to with you. It's time for you to know what I want, and that I'm not going to be the nice patient guy who pretends he doesn't care."

"This is a huge change."

"I needed time. I've had time, and I'm ready."

The music turned down to a slow number, and he tugged her out of the booth. "Come on, let's dance."

He led her onto the dance-floor with several other couples. Baker pulled her into his arms, and she wrapped hers around his neck, staring up at him.

"How is my date?" he asked.

"The best I ever had."

"You're comparing me?"

"Not comparing you. Just comparing how I feel."

He grabbed her ass, pulling her close. The rock hard ridge of his cock pressed against her stomach.

Millie liked this side of Baker. He wasn't holding back. Every time he looked at her, she couldn't help but feel beautiful.

He didn't look at any other women. His focus was on her, and she loved it.

The world could have stopped moving for her. For once in her life, she was happy, and she didn't want anyone to destroy that.

"Millie," he said.

"Yeah."

She looked up at him. The moment she did, he pressed his lips against hers, and his tongue ran across wanting to gain access.

"Open for me, Millie."

Opening her mouth, she moaned as his tongue plunged inside. Touching hers to his, he squeezed her ass even tighter, rubbing his cock against her.

She didn't know how much time passed, only that the song had changed from a slow number to a fast number.

"Do you want to get out of here?" he asked.

"Would you like to come back to my place?"

"Yeah, I would."

"I'm not ready for—"

He silenced her with a kiss. "I would never pressure you. I want you, Millie. Only when you're ready, and I'm a good guy. Doesn't mean I can't tease you with all of this hotness."

Cupping his cheek, she ran her thumb across his lips. "Don't stop. Promise me."

"Babe, it's a guarantee. I'm here for you, and you alone. We'll go at your pace. Just know that as far as I'm concerned we're exclusive."

"Yes. I wouldn't cheat, Baker. That's not the kind of woman I am."

"Come on, let's get out of here."

After they paid for their food, they left.

****

Lash wrapped his arms around his woman, breathing in her vanilla scent. "You owe me big time."

Angel giggled. "Why?"

"You didn't warn me how crazy those kids can be. They were all screaming, and making noises of all of the animals. Fucking crazy."

"Even Anthony?"

He knew Angel was worried about how quiet their son was. Anthony was a good kid, but he'd always been a bit of a loner. Angel worried that the club life was affecting him, and had even asked if she should keep him away to see if it was their influence. Lash had talked with Anthony for a long time that night. His son was simply content with his own company. He adored the other kids, but again, Anthony was just different.

"Even Anthony. You should have heard him making pig noises with Daisy."

"That's good to know. I want him to have a

normal life, Lash."

"He will. There's nothing wrong with The Skulls. We're just our own people, Angel."

"I know, I know. I just worry is all. I want Anthony to make his own mind, and to know what he wants to be."

"He will." Lash kissed her neck. "Stop worrying. Daisy will bring him out of his skin. Haven't you seen how he watches her?"

"Yeah, he likes her to read to him."

Lash chuckled. "I think it's a little more than that. Did you get Millie ready?"

"I helped. I adore her. She's a little confusing at times."

"How do you mean?"

"Some days I get the feeling that she just wants to belong, and to be part of all of us. Other days it's like she is almost afraid of getting close."

"I've never seen Baker look so happy. You should have seen him. He was even whistling."

"The club is changing, Lash. Are you happy about that?"

"Years ago, before I met you, I couldn't imagine The Skulls being any different. Now, after everything we've faced, the people we've lost, the shit that has happened, I don't want to go back to the way things were. This is the club. We've grown up. We've got a family, and with that, we have to learn to adapt."

"You don't miss the drug runs, or the guns? The action, the stuff that almost got you killed?"

Lash turned her around to face him. "I nearly lost you, Angel. Not just once either. We lost a baby, and I nearly lost you. I wouldn't trade that shit for you. Never. You're my life, my heart, everything. If I can't have you, Angel, then I don't want anyone else. That's it for me."

Tears filled her eyes, and he wiped them away as they spilled down her cheeks. "Sometimes, Lash, you say the most beautiful things."

"My wife's been showing me how to be a better man."

"She sounds awesome."

"She really is." He kissed her lips, and that first touch was like the first time, every single time. Angel was his entire life. Lash would fight heaven and hell to make her safe. He'd nearly lost her so many times, in so many different ways, he just couldn't do it. He couldn't go back to the way The Skulls were. As President of the club, he was making changes that he was determined to see stick.

****

Sally went onto her toes trying to reach up to grab the box of fettuccine but it was just out of her reach, and it was really starting to hurt seeing as she only had one foot to use.

"Here, let me," Steven said, reaching up behind her, grabbing a box.

"Thank you. I've been trying to grab that for ages." She held it up. "I'm starving. Do you want to join me in some fettuccine alfredo?"

"If you're cooking, I'm eating."

"Lacey is a horrible cook, so I learned how to do it." Sally already had the other ingredients out of the fridge. It was late and her knee was hurting, but she was determined to cook herself some food without the use of her crutches. The drive back from college had been longer than she anticipated. By the time they hit Fort Wills, Drew hadn't had much time. He dropped her off at the club with her bags.

"I've tried some of her food. Woman should be banned from eating." Steven didn't move away. He stood beside her as she started to cook.

Pain started to radiate from her knee, up her thigh. She rubbed the spot, trying not to draw attention to what she was doing.

Sally noticed Steven took over with all the heavy lifting, draining the pasta as she finished up the creamy cheese sauce.

By the time they finished, Steven carried their food to the table, and she lowered herself down, rubbing at her leg.

"Drew didn't stop off for food?" Steven asked.

"We didn't have much time. His family was waiting for him. I don't mind."

"Still, any guy could see you're in pain."

"It's not his fault."

"No, it's our fault."

She glared at him. "Are you here to do a pity party or something?" Sally asked.

"Just speaking the truth."

"I don't consider that the truth. It wasn't the club's fault, and I'm not blaming anyone. It is what it is." She truly didn't blame the club. No, her anger was at the asshole who did it, who also happened to be dead. So, she was more than happy with it. "What's wrong with you anyway?"

"Nothing."

"You're miserable, and that's not an attractive quality."

"I worry about you, Sally. Always have. Always will."

She smiled. "Steven, I remember a time when you were worried about me having a crush on you. Believe me, you don't have to worry. The doctors have said that I'll have pain, and some days it'll be worse than others. Please, don't worry."

"Do you have a crush on me anymore?" he asked.

Sally stared at him. "What?"

"You heard me."

Her heart started to pound as she stared at the man opposite her. She *did* have a crush on him. A few years ago she'd heard him talking to another club member, she couldn't remember who, and he'd sounded a little disgusted at the thought of her having feelings. So she'd told him that she didn't have a crush.

"I don't see what you're hoping to achieve."

"I want to know the truth, Sally. Do you have feelings for me, or have you moved on?"

Before she got a chance to answer, Whizz and Lacey entered the kitchen, surrounding her.

"You're back," Lacey said, pressing kisses to her cheek.

She scrunched up her face as Lacey kept on kissing her.

"I get it, I get it, you missed me."

"Totally missed you, and wish you had never left us."

Kiss, kiss, kiss.

Whizz kissed the top of Sally's head and squeezed her shoulder.

She didn't know if she was happy with them interrupting her and Steven or not. When she looked at him, she saw that he was staring at her, waiting.

Holy crap, what was she going to do?

Chapter Four

Entering her home, Millie turned on the lights, and waited for Baker to enter. Closing and locking the door, she made her way up the stairs. Other than The Skulls women that afternoon, no one else had been in her home.

"Do you like living and working in the same place?"

"I do. I love being my own boss. I couldn't stand the thought of taking orders from someone I don't like."

She turned the light on and moved some of the clothes that Lacey had thrown to one side on the sofa. Wrapping it up, she threw it into her room. "Sorry. The whole afternoon was spent going through all my clothes."

"I don't mind. You see being part of The Skulls, the old ladies come with it."

"I find that term weird. Old ladies." She tucked some hair behind her ear, and walked into the kitchen. "Do you want a coffee or a tea, or maybe some juice?" she asked.

"I'll have a coffee." He was standing right behind her.

She gasped as he wrapped his arms around her waist and pulled her close. In the next second he had her pressed against the fridge and his lips were on hers.

Her pussy went wet as his tongue plundered her mouth. She was so shocked by the sudden attack on her senses that at first she didn't kiss him back. He rubbed his cock against her stomach, and she moaned, finally giving in to her need. Holding him close, she sank her fingers into his hair, holding onto him.

As suddenly as the kiss started, it stopped.

He pulled away just enough for his breath to fan her face. "I didn't mean for that to happen."

"That's a shame. I rather liked it."

Baker moaned. "I'm trying to be the good guy here."

"You are the good guy. I'm not ready for it to go any further. I've never seen this side of you, Baker, and I want to get to know him before anything else happens."

He stroked her hair and stepped away. "I'll go and take a seat."

Her lips tingled from the kiss, and she couldn't wipe the smile off her face. Everything was out of a fairytale. Well, a biker fairytale, but she loved it.

She made them both a coffee, and made her way into the sitting room. Baker was standing beside her book collection. She was a sucker for romances and cookbooks. Other than that, there was nothing else on her shelves.

"Angel has similar collections," he said, turning toward her.

"I know. She was the one that recommended some of those books." She put the coffee onto coasters and took a seat, watching him.

This was the first time a guy was in her home, and especially a guy she actually liked.

He moved and took a seat beside her. Resting her hand on her head, she smiled at him.

"I enjoyed tonight, and I enjoyed that kiss."

"Thank you, for giving me a chance. I know it mustn't have been easy for you to do."

"It wasn't. I believe you, and I wanted to go out on a date with you."

"You know from the first moment I saw you, I knew you were going to be trouble."

"You didn't say a lot if I remember," she said,

smiling. "The Skulls had ordered a lot of gifts, and you were there to help bring them into the club."

"I was. I wanted you there and then."

"You wore your wedding band."

"I did. Katie was still with me."

Millie stared into his eyes, and she no longer saw the pain that had once been in his eyes. He really had moved on.

Baker took hold of her hand and stared down at her plain fingers. To her they were fat chubby fingers. Brian had complained that he'd have to expand his grandmother's ring because they were too big.

Wow, twice in one night she'd thought of her ex.

Maybe with Baker moving on, it was time for her to do so as well.

"You look sad. What's up, baby?"

"Nothing. Just thinking about the past, and another lifetime. It's nothing. I'm going to move on, and completely forget about it."

"If you want to move on, what do you think of making out?"

"I think I'd really like to do that."

"Have you ever done it before?" he asked.

"No."

"Not even with your ex?"

"No. Like I said, I thought he was a sweet guy who was considerate. I didn't know at the time that he was screwing someone else. I haven't made out with anyone, nor have been felt up before."

Baker's hands moved to her hips, and Millie squealed as he moved her over his lap so that she was straddling his hips.

"Then we've got to rectify that."

His hands moved up and down her back, grabbing onto her ass.

"Wow, you're very grabby."

"You've not seen anything yet."

His hands moved from her ass, going up to her hair and tugging on the strands. He claimed her mouth, and she cupped his face, kissing him back with a passion that started her. This time, she plunged her tongue into his mouth. Grinding her pussy onto his cock, she wished there weren't any clothes between them.

"Fuck, baby, you don't know what you're doing to me."

"I can feel it, Baker. I don't have a clue what I'm doing."

"You're doing everything right." He pulled her hair, and she followed his hands. Baker sucked on her neck, sliding his tongue down. "I could quite easily sink inside your tight pussy right now, but I'm not going to. Instead, I'm going to touch you. Is that okay, Millie?"

"Yes, hell yes," she said.

He flicked open the catch of her jeans, and his hand slid inside, touching her pussy. That first touch made her jump, and then his fingers were moving through her slit, touching her clit, stroking her.

She jerked back to stare into his eyes. Baker didn't stop. Two fingers explored her clit, running back and forth so lightly.

"You're wet for me, baby."

"Oh, God," she said, closing her eyes, arching against his fingers, she thrust her pussy onto his fingers.

"Ride me, Millie."

Her shirt gave way, and she opened her eyes in time to see him working the buttons.

Seconds later her bra was fingered open and his lips were on her breasts, sucking on her nipples.

It was all too much.

There, on Baker's lap, with his fingers rubbing

her clit, Millie found her first orgasm.

When it was over, she collapsed against his neck, panting.

"That was the hottest thing I've ever seen."

She chuckled. "That's my first."

"I'm honored to be your first. Whenever you need me, just give me a call, and I'll come running."

"Are you offering to be my go-to dildo?" she asked, a little startled.

"I'm offering to be your anything."

She pushed her hair out of her face, and Baker removed his hands.

Millie watched as he sucked his fingers.

"You taste beautiful."

Words failed her.

One date, and he already had his hands in her pants. There was no way she was going to be able to hold out for long. She wanted him as much as he wanted her.

****

"Someone is in a good mood," Lash said.

Baker smiled as he walked in for coffee. It had been a good night, a good date, and even though he'd not wanted to leave her alone, he had.

"I am." He poured himself some coffee that always seemed to be waiting. "My date went really well with Millie last night. The girls did an awesome job. I think they helped me crack her a little bit."

Millie had been more open last night than any other time.

"Crack her? What the hell did you do?" Lash asked.

"I found out that she was once engaged. Shocked the shit out of me."

"For real? Is this like what happened to Kelsey?"

"Nah, completely different. Millie caught the guy

she was going to marry cheating on her, on her wedding day. Asshole." Baker didn't like the guy, and he didn't even know who he was.

"Oh, do I hear some detective work needed?" Whizz asked, entering the kitchen.

Out of all of The Skulls, Whizz was the best of the best. He was a computer genius, a nerd of the highest order, and a brilliant hacker. He gathered information faster than fucking lightning.

"I don't know."

"Her name is Millie Levy, right?" Baker nodded. "I can have all of her past information to you in a nice neat little file, just for you."

Baker thought about it.

He wanted to know everything there was to know about the woman he wanted. Millie, she was special to him. There wasn't a moment that went by where he wasn't thinking about her.

"No."

Whizz stared. "Are you sure? I can do it, and she'll never have to know. Completely top secret shit."

"No. I'm not going to do that to her. Whatever she wants me to know, I'll find out through her. Some things are better left not known." He trusted her, and the last thing he wanted to do was pry into her past. Everything she wanted him to know, she'd simply tell him.

"You know it's about to get crazy. Kids are due down in minutes," Lash said, moaning. "Why, oh, why did we agree to deal with them in bulk in the club around trip season?"

"Because it does actually work," Whizz said. "One by one, we get through it. Also, it's easy."

"I don't know. Have you seen how much food we get through?"

"As a club, we get through loads," Baker said. "Anyway, I'm out."

"Where are you going?" Lash asked.

"I'm going to go and visit my girl."

"Is this what you did for your first wife?" Whizz asked.

"Pretty much. I was always around her, and she couldn't get rid of me."

He saw Lash and Whizz shared a look.

"What?"

"You didn't go crazy on us. Whenever we mentioned your wife in the past, you went crazy. Wow, you must really be ready to move on."

Baker shrugged. "I told you I was happy, and I'm ready. Now, I've got to go and convince the girl of my dreams to be my old lady."

"It's not exactly a good way to ask her," Lash said.

"Yeah, women really don't like the whole old comment," Whizz said. "Believe me. It stops you getting head, or any kind of action at all."

"I bet with Lacey, you nearly lose your dick, right?"

Whizz thought about it. "Yep, pretty much. Good thing for me, Lacey has really sensitive tits, so we're both equal."

Baker shook his head. "I really don't need to know this crap, okay? I'm happy pretending none of you fuck."

"Actually, we do it a lot. Have you seen my old lady? Angel is fucking perfect."

Now he knew they were doing it on purpose. Lash would never, ever talk about his woman.

"Ugh, you're both doing this on purpose. When I bring Millie around, you both better be on your good behavior."

"You know what would be good for her?" Lash asked.

"What?"

"Some of your awesome baking. Sort of, 'hi, Millie, I want your pussy, here is a brioche loaf. I made this, spent all day doing it'."

Baker stared at his Prez. "And how exactly would you know brioche takes all day to do?"

"I told him," Angel said, entering the kitchen with Chloe on her hip. "He even helped me to do it. I'd safely say that my boy can make the best brioche loaf there is. He even filled it with chocolate chips."

"Is that right? Maybe I should take your load, and let Millie have a taste."

"Go right ahead," Lash said. "She'll fall right into my hands, wouldn't she, baby?"

"Any woman who tasted your brioche would." Angel kissed his lips. "But you're mine, Lash." She turned to Baker. "You'll be making your own girl brioche. Not my man."

"Don't worry. I'm happy to do it all myself." He winked at her. "But I'd be happy to take you off his hands."

Lash growled. "If you respect your life, you'll stop trying to poach my woman."

"Think about that when you speak of Millie. Same feeling, brother," Baker said, glaring at him.

"Excellent. I can't wait for her to be part of the club. You'll stop being a pain in the ass. Love you, brother, but you've got the worst scowl in the world."

Angel placed Chloe in Lash's arms.

"Daddy," Chloe said.

"Hello, sweetie. Do we think Baker is miserable?" Lash stuck his lip out, looking all miserable.

"Yes! Baker sad." Chloe copied pulling a face.

"That's not fair. She'll do anything you say." Baker walked away laughing. "Whatever. I'm heading out to see Millie, and try not to get into too much trouble."

"We're trouble with a capital T," Lash said.

Baker heard them all laughing, and he made his way out of the club toward his bike. Straddling the beauty that had brought him to the club, and to his future, he turned over the ignition, loving the growl of the machine. "That's right, beauty."

Pulling away from the parking lot, he headed out toward the town of Fort Wills. He made a quick stop at the florist in town before moving toward Millie's shop. The sign saying she was open was already displayed, and he entered in time to see her bent over with her full round ass begging for him to touch.

"Fuck, baby, that is a beautiful sight."

She let out a little squeal and stood. "Baker, I wasn't expecting you."

Placing the flowers down on the counter, he moved toward her, and tugged her into his arms. "I've wanted to do this all morning." Slamming his lips down on hers, he gave her a searing kiss.

He finally released her, seconds later, giving her a chance to breathe.

"Wow," she said, shooting him a dazzling smile. "What happened to the real Baker?"

"This is the real me, baby."

She tilted her head, staring at him. "That's strange. I've never seen this Baker before." She touched his chin, turning his face this way and that. "Nah, it can't be you. This man has to be an imposter."

"You've never seen me like this before, but I can promise you, this is me." He ran his hands down her back, enjoying the feel of her in his arms. She felt so right that he knew he'd fucked up by keeping her at arm's length.

"I think I like this guy."

"Good. He's here to stay."

She bit her lip. "For real?"

"Yes, for real, and I was thinking. What do you say you and I go away for a little bit?"

"Away? Like a vacation?"

"Yes. You, me, and just each other. Time."

Millie stared into his eyes. "Is there going to be some kind of special catch to this?"

"No catch at all. I've seen how time alone has helped Charlotte and Gash. I think it's only fair we give it a fair shot as well."

"I'd like that. I really would."

"When do you think we can do it? I can talk with Lash, and we can organize some time away."

"How about this weekend? I'm my own boss. We can go wherever you want to go."

He pressed a kiss to her lips. "Consider it done."

"I feel like I'm dreaming."

"This is not a dream." He kissed her one last time, and left the shop.

A vacation away was exactly what they needed.

Chapter Five

Angel winced as the tip of the blade cut her finger. Sucking the wound into her mouth, she glared down at the brownies. They were perfectly cooked, only the blade was too damn sharp.

"You okay?"

She turned to see Tiny leaning against the doorway.

"Yeah, I'm good. I just cut my finger. I'm a klutz."

"You know you don't have to keep every single cookie jar and cake display full with goods."

Angel baked roughly four times a week to keep the clubhouse supplied in sweet stuff. It was strange. She would rather they eat the baking she provided rather than buying it. Also, she liked the random tips that Baker gave her when he was in the mood to share. He was such a talented guy. She did believe his talents were wasted, and even asked Lash to try to convince him to open up his own bakery. They had been planning to do it, but Baker had told them no. Now that he was moving on, and things seemed to be going well with Millie, she wondered if he'd consider it again.

"I like doing it. You guys are my family, and I like taking care of you all."

"Eva never did it, nor did Patricia before her." Patricia was his first wife who'd died of cancer. She was the mother to Tate.

"I know I'm not what you imagined as an old lady for Lash." For the longest time she'd felt Tiny's judgment. She never told Lash about it. Her husband was very protective, and he would more likely hurt Tiny for inadvertently hurting her. "I try my hardest to be a good wife, a good old lady."

Tiny stepped into the room. "Lash wanted you from the first moment he saw you. Your dad, he owed the club, and we had you…" He stopped. "Angel, I'm not perfect, okay. I did things that even now I regret. I cheated on my first wife, and I kept Eva at arm's length. I caused this club a lot of bad shit, and I got us out of it, and back into it. Some would say I'm not a very good man, but I do my best."

"You've been the best, Tiny. You shouldn't think anything else."

"Still, I know I could do better. Lash has had the club completely without any enemies for over three years. Look at this place. It's thriving better than I've ever seen it. Everyone is so happy, and you know what? I'm happy. This is how I always hoped the club would be. Only I was never good enough to get it that way. I didn't have the vision that Lash had. I have the ideals, and the hopes. He's been determined to make this place a home." Tiny took hold of her hand. His large hand completely swamped hers. Tiny was a deadly force, and Lash had warned her to never cross him. "Angel, I couldn't be more proud than if you were my own daughter. You've helped mold Lash into the man he is today. Without you, he wouldn't be the same. Don't ever believe for a second that you're not good enough. I'm the one that is not good enough. You are exactly like your name, Angel. You're an angel." He leaned forward and pressed a kiss to her cheek.

Tears sprang to her eyes as warmth spread throughout her entire body.

"Thank you."

She dropped her head, unable to let him see her tears.

"No, Angel. Thank you."

"You're making my woman cry?" Lash asked.

Angel burst out laughing. "They're happy tears. You know. I tell you about them all the time."

"Still doesn't mean I like them."

Tiny stepped back. "She nicked her finger. You might what to look at it. I'd be careful of those knives if I was you."

Seconds later he was gone from the kitchen, and Angel couldn't stop smiling.

"What is it, babe?" Lash asked.

"He likes me, Lash. He actually likes me."

"Of course he does. I'll hurt anyone who doesn't like you. You're my girl."

"No, it's not that. I've always been weaker. I'm not like Tate, or Lacey, or Prue."

"I don't want to be married to any of them. First, Tate is like a sister, yuck. Lacey is too damn scary, and I'd probably have my balls chopped off before the end of the day. Prue is not my type. She argues too much. Besides, I love you, Angel. No other woman would ever compare to you." He kissed her lips, and any concern melted away.

****

Tate watched her husband where he was fiddling with his bike again. They weren't at the club, but at their home. It was strange how much time they spent away from the club nowadays. She stared at the scars decorating his face. He'd gotten them during an attack, when his bike blew up. Tate remembered being terrified because everyone thought he was dead. She was a bitch most of the time, and knew a lot of people couldn't stand her. When it came to Murphy, she never wanted anything to happen to him. She loved him so much that it hurt even the thought of anything happening to him. For a long time after he'd gotten the scars, he wouldn't look at her, or even bed her. He'd withdrawn completely from her, not that she'd told anyone at the club. It had taken her some time to find out what was bothering him. Everything went back to his scars. He truly thought he was ugly and no longer deserved her. Tate's heart had broken a little that day.

She was a first class bitch. She knew it, accepted it. When it came to Murphy, the love she had for him would rival no other. He was the love of her life, and the fact he thought a few scars would scare her away had broken her.

"Mommy," Isabella said, tugging on her skirt.

Bending down, Tate picked her little girl up, smiling at her. "Shall we go and see what Daddy is up to?"

"Yeah!"

Giggling, she walked out toward her man.

"How are my two beautiful girls?" Murphy asked without even looking up.

"How did you know it was us, Daddy?" Isabella asked.

He looked up, and tapped his nose. "A Daddy always knows." He stood up, and Isabella reached out for him. "How is my little girl doing?"

"I want you to play with me."

"In a bit, sweetie."

"Now, please. I got a tea party. Simon's playing when he gets home."

"Poor Simon," Murphy said. "Run in, and get it ready. I'll be in in a minute. Maybe we can get Mommy to pull that banoffee pie out of fridge. Let us all have a slice early."

"Yes!" Isabella ran into the house screaming and cheering.

"You spoil her."

"Ah, I spoil both of my girls." Murphy pulled her in close, gripping her ass. "So how is my big girl?"

She scrunched up her nose. "That just sounds wrong, Daddy." She raised her brow, and Murphy shook his head.

"Yeah. There's no way I'll ever be your daddy."

Tate burst out laughing. "Sometimes I wonder about us. How we got here."

"A lot of hard work, and scars." Murphy touched his face, and she sighed.

"Your scars are never going to be a problem to me. I love you, Murphy, and your wicked tongue."

"You really can't go long without my wicked tongue, can you?"

"Why would I want to? It's all mine." Cupping his face, Tate pressed her lips to his, sliding her tongue across them until he opened. Plunging inside, she felt the stirring of his cock, and moaned. Neither of them could do anything about that right now.

"You know how to tease me."

"There's something I want to ask you." Taking his hand, she made her way toward the kitchen. She stopped at the sitting room. "I'm just going to cut that pie, baby, okay?"

"Yes, Mommy."

Isabella was a good little girl. Being a mother to her was a dream to Tate. She'd always wanted to be a mother for as long as she could remember.

"What is it?" Murphy asked.

She grabbed the pie from the fridge, and turned toward Murphy. "I've been having a lot of thoughts just lately, and there's something I want to ask you."

"The suspense is killing me."

"The club is safe. The Skulls and Chaos Bleeds, nothing bad has happened in nearly four years now. So, I was wondering what you'd think of possibly relocating."

"You want to move?"

"Yes and no. I want to move and I want to stay here. Fort Wills, it's in my blood. It's our family home."

"I don't know where this is coming from?"

"Ugh, it's hard for me right now to understand. I love you, Murphy. You've done wonders for the club, but if you would like a fresh start, then I'm with you. If you'd like to move, and for us to just be a family of four, I'd like you to know you don't have to stay here. Just recently I've seen how sad you are. You're not happy here. I don't know if it's me or something—"

Murphy silenced her with a kiss. "Shut up, babe."

"I've been happy for so long. You're all I ever wanted. This and you, and the kids. All of it is my dream. This is my fantasy, and I get to live it every single day." Tears filled her eyes and started to fall down her cheeks. "Damn, I promised myself I wouldn't cry."

"Baby, what has brought all this on?"

"I've been so selfish. All of my life, I used my mother's passing as a way of getting what I wanted. The poor little biker princess lost her mommy, and now, I don't know. I guess I've finally grown up, and I see the error of my ways. I see it now more than ever before, and I don't like what I see. When I look in the mirror, I'm not who I wanted to be." She pressed her lips together. "I see my mother, and, Murphy, she wasn't a very nice woman. I'm not a very nice woman. I want to be better than her." She wiped away the tears, no longer able to stand them. "So, whatever you want to do, or wherever you want to go, I'm here, and I'm willing."

****

Friday morning, Baker whistled as he parked the car outside of Millie's home. He'd spent the past week organizing for them to go away, and he intended for this to be the best time away. Knocking on her door, he stood back as a second later she came out with a case.

"Is that all you have packed?"

"Yes. We're going away for the week right?"

"Yes."

"Then this is it. I've always been a light traveler." She had her hair pulled back into a ponytail.

He grabbed her case and dumped it into the trunk of the car. "So, I couldn't exactly go far."

"Alright, so where are you thinking?"

"We're heading to Vegas, baby. Alex let me have a room at his hotel." A few years ago, Alex had remained a permanent resident of Fort Wills, leaving his Vegas casino behind. However, he still owned the casino, but he left it to a manager that he trusted.

"Yay."

"Yeah, so stopping off at the airport, and then guess who is meeting us at Vegas to take us to the casino?" he asked.

"I have absolutely no idea."

"Butch. He's coming to meet us."

"Oh, I don't think I've met him before," she said, frowning.

"Don't worry. He's a good guy that has been out in Vegas for awhile. He came home to help the club during Andrew's anger." He kissed her hand, tugging her close. "Let's go and have some fun."

For the next few hours, neither of them really got a chance to talk. From parking the car, he carried both of their cases through the airport, and then it was a waiting game. Baker sent a text to Butch, to make sure he was ready to pick them up. Alex had said that he, Sunshine, and their baby girl, Candice, may be paying a visit to go and see his son, Michael.

Yeah, that was a little drama. Cheryl, Butch's old

lady, had had a child with Alex, who was also a member of The Skulls. She hadn't known that Alex was a club member, and when she met Butch, Michael had been nearly five, or a little older. Baker couldn't remember the complete ins and outs of it.

Five to six hours later, they were touching down in Vegas, and that had been a damn good turn around, especially as there was also a little delay in the flights. Holding Millie's hand, he grabbed their luggage, and found Butch waiting for them with Michael beside him.

"Hey," he said, pulling Baker in for a hug.

"Hey yourself." Baker hugged his brother, and pulled away. "Millie, this is Butch. Butch, this is the gorgeous Millie."

"Ah, I remember you now. I couldn't remember your name. I'm so sorry."

Butch shook her hand and took a deep breath. "So, you're heading toward the casino?"

"Yeah. Alex said I could use his penthouse room. It was kind of a last minute organizing. You know Charlotte and Gash have been able to find each other after everything they've been through. I'm hoping to do the same with Millie."

"Is my dad coming?" Michael asked, drawing attention to him.

"Alex has said he's going to head out with Candice and Sunshine."

"I get to see my sister?"

"Yes," Butch said, smiling. "Let's get this show on the road. I don't want your mom angry at me for missing dinner."

Michael shook his head. "She's making grilled cheese."

"Oh, my favorite."

They made their way out of the airport toward

Butch's car.

"We should all have dinner sometime."

"Sure, we'd love to," Baker said.

He chatted with Butch on the way to the casino, aware of Millie silent by his side. She was staring out of the window, and he was worried that he was making her feel left out.

Butch offered to help him with his bags, but seeing as they only had two, Baker didn't see the point.

Within minutes they were inside Alex's penthouse suite, and even Baker was a little shocked.

"Wow, this is Alex, club Alex?" Millie asked.

"Yeah. He has this big ranch house outside of Fort Wills. It's like a mini mansion. I never knew it was like this."

"This is amazing. My family would have loved something like this."

"Your family?"

"Yeah," she said.

"You've never spoken of your family."

"It's kind of hard to do when you don't exactly speak *to* them." She tucked some hair behind her ear. The ponytail she wore that morning was long gone, and he noticed she did look a little tired.

"They're still alive then?"

"My family?" He nodded. "Of course. I mean, I never said they were dead. They're just, I'm not exactly in their good graces at the moment."

"If you don't want to talk about it, that's okay, but I don't mind listening though."

She groaned. "It's complicated. Erm, this is supposed to be our time for each other."

"I want to know everything about you. Absolutely everything."

"How about we talk, and unpack? I don't want

wrinkled clothing." Millie grabbed her case and headed toward one of the bedrooms.

"I was hoping we'd share a room."

"Baker?"

"I know you're a virgin, and this is all probably completely scary for you. I get it, babe, I do. I just want to hold you. Is that okay? I want to hold you."

"No funny business?"

"Only if you beg me to."

She chuckled. "I won't ask."

"We'll see."

Opening the door to the main master bedroom, he switched on the lights. The bed was fit for a damn orgy it was that big. Baker had some ideas of how to use it. Of course, he would never make Millie feel uncomfortable.

"Family, spill."

"Ugh, my family are wealthy. They're not this kind of wealthy, but in the town where I used to live, they were one of the top five wealthiest families. They owned a factory or something. Anyway, with it came the mindset that their daughters would marry well."

"Daughters? You have a sister?"

Her cheeks heated. "Yeah, er, her name is Bethany."

"I take it you weren't close."

Millie held a shirt and sat down. "Do you remember me telling you that on my wedding day that I walked into the guy that I was supposed to be marrying, and he was having sex with someone that really wasn't me?"

"I wouldn't forget that."

"The woman was my sister. Bethany been screwing Brian for a long time, and she enjoyed it."

"Is she younger than you?"

"No, older in fact, by five years."

"She was breaking the law?"

"Brian wasn't exactly complaining. I doubt he'd have been complaining when my sister screwed his brains out. She's the hot one. The one that all guys want to be with. She's blonde, slim, beautiful."

"And I bet mean."

"Some would agree. Others, not so much."

"She hurt you."

Millie let out a breath, staring at the wall past his shoulder. "Bethany was brought up to believe she can have anything. Clicks her fingers, and ta-da, it's done. A new pet, she could have it. My cat, she'd have it, the family dog wasn't so nice to her, they sold it, and got another one, or worse, took it to the pet rescue center."

"Wow."

"Growing up, I learned not to get attached to anything, or anyone. Life is a hell of a lot easier when you're not losing something you love."

"Did you love Brian?"

"I thought I did. He was supposed to by my high school sweetheart. He came to me, said all the right things. It's really humiliating when I think back to it."

"It's not your fault."

"No? When I left, I cried so much that I would give myself migraines. I wasn't crying for Brian. I was crying for myself. I wanted to make my parents proud, and to prove to everyone that the chubby, mousy, brown haired girl could get a good man. She could live happily ever after, and from the start, it was all a lie." There were no tears, only acceptance.

"You can have that."

"No, I can't. It's delusional for women like us to even think that way. Isn't that what everyone says? If you've got curves, or a bit of weight. You're unlovable? Undesirable? I've never known true passion, not really."

Baker stepped right up close to her. Tugging the shirt out of her hands, he pulled her to her feet. Sinking his fingers into her hair, he pressed his lips to hers. "Passion? You don't think you've ever experienced it? What about with me?"

Before he gave her time to answer, he claimed her lips, tightening his hold on the back of her head, to keep her in place. Making love to her mouth took on a whole new meaning. He didn't want her to feel like she didn't deserve love or passion. She did. He'd been a complete asshole for holding out so long. He'd been so consumed with his own mourning that he'd never considered Millie dealing with her own kind of pain, and she was. She was in a lot of it, and he'd been so selfish with his own.

He was determined to rectify that situation.

Millie was never going to feel that way again.

It was not only a promise he was going to make to himself, it was a damn vow.

****

The kiss was completely different from everything she'd ever experienced. The passion, the lust, the need, all combined together to leave her breathless. Millie never intended to speak the truth, to release her feelings out for him to know.

Baker broke the kiss, pressing a quick peck to her nose. "That was just a taster, baby."

She loved it when he called her babe or baby. She loved all the sweet little names that he'd called her. They were a nice change from fatty, fatso, ugly, or useless. That was the one she hated the most, useless. She always accepted the other comments, or criticism. She was fat, and she wasn't beautiful. The opposite of beauty is ugliness, so that was her. She accepted it, and like Bethany had told her many times, she needed to learn her station. The fats and the ugly people, stayed out of the way.

Bethany was one of the worst sisters, and of the most horrible people Millie had ever known. Not all people were like her sister. The past six years, since she'd known The Skulls, had taught her that the most amazing people came in all different sizes, slim or not.

"What's going on inside that head of yours?"

"Nothing. I'm just shocked by the kiss." Her lips tingled.

"Your lips look nice, red, and puffy. Exactly how well kissed lips should look. Tell me about the rest of your family?"

"Nothing much to tell. My mom and dad spoiled Bethany, and myself. We were both spoiled girls."

"Why are you nice, and your sister sounds like a dragon?"

Millie laughed. "Even though we were spoilt, Bethany and I had always been different. She was the oldest so she had our parents' attention straight away. When I came along, they were too busy, and Bethany fit into their world perfectly. At the time I was just a baby. I could do nothing more than scream, eat, barf, and poop. So I got left with my grandma. She was a lovely woman."

"Really?"

"On my father's side." Millie giggled. "She started out as my granddad's mistress, and when he grew tired of convention, he divorced the woman he was with who he hated, and married my grandma. They lived happily, and had my dad. Anyway, it was the talk of the town, and from what I remember, my dad hated it. He decided he'd put the respect and honor back into the name. Seeing as my granddad left all of the fortune to my grandma, he couldn't just toss her out on the street."

"His own mother?" Baker asked.

"Oh yes. The Levy family is quite scandalous, or it was immediately after my grandfather's death, and his will."

"You've got to tell me more."

Millie sighed. "You really want to know this?"

"I want to know the woman that helped to raise the woman I'm with."

They finished putting their clothes away and headed into the kitchen. "Alex really thought of everything didn't he? A kitchen, a bedroom. The only thing I don't see is a way to do laundry."

"He always had it dry cleaned."

"Oh, that's why." Millie smiled. "It's a really beautiful penthouse."

"Stop changing the subject. Come on, I want to know some more."

She rolled her eyes and took a seat beside him on the long sofa. "Fine, fine. I was dumped with my grandparents, and when I was twelve, my grandfather passed away. I loved spending time with them. My sister believed they were too old and boring. Me, I loved it. Grandma knew how to bake the most delicious, tender chocolate chip cookies. I loved them. I'd spend hours in the kitchen with her, baking, cooking, and on occasion, canning. Anyway, from what I recall, Dad hated the reputation she had. A slut, a home-wrecker, and some other horrible things. If Granddad ever heard stuff said, he would handle it." She smiled. "He was a true gentleman, and I'd always hoped to have a guy like him. Someone who wasn't afraid to stand up for who he loved."

"He sounds like a good guy."

"He really was."

"Get back to the juicy story."

She chuckled. "Okay, I spent all my time with them. When I was twelve Granddad had a heart attack. A big one, and he didn't make it. Died within hours of it." She took a breath. It had been years ago, but it still hurt. "The day after, Dad kicked Grandma out of the house. Told her she wasn't welcome with them anymore, and that he wasn't going to have riffraff plaguing the Levy name. This was his mother, and yet he acted like she was nothing but the hired help. It was so horrible to see. Anyway, a week later at Grandfather's will, everything changed. Dad had believed that he'd inherit everything. Why not? He was the legal heir to the Levy fortune. He'd been trained to take over, and with it, he could do whatever the hell he wanted." Millie smiled. "I think my granddad knew what would happen, and he changed his will, or he always had his will so that Grandma would inherit absolutely everything."

"She did?" Baker asked.

"Yeah. The fortune was hers, the business was hers, the houses, the cars, the furniture. Every single thing belonged to her, and if my dad kicked her out, then in the will it was decreed my father would have nothing, would own nothing, and it would be time for him to take his own place in the world."

"Wow!"

Millie giggled. "For the first time in my life, I got to see the fear in my parents' eyes. They lived on my grandparents' good graces. Grandma came back home, and everything changed. I mean everything. My parents tried to spend every moment with her, I even think they tried to have it decreed that my grandfather wasn't mentally fit to do such a will."

"There was no way they could change it?"

"None. Grandma is and will always be the sole owner until she picks someone to take over, and it may not be my dad."

"Do you still talk to her?"

"All the time. After I moved out, she went to Italy, and lives there most of the year, only returning when she needs to."

"When the shop closes for random weeks, is that where you go?"

"Yes, I go to see her. She's seventy-nine now, but is still so damn healthy. I love her. My family hated me for that. They thought I'd turned her against them."

"I do not like your family."

"You're not the only ones that feel that way. That's my family, Baker. Now you know everything about me. Every little detail."

"Why do I feel there's so much to know about you?"

"I don't know. I'm just me." Her stomach rumbled. "And now it's time for dinner. I'm starving."

"Come on, let's go and get some food."

She made her way into the kitchen, wondering what she'd find. Opening up the fridge, she was shocked to see it was fully stocked. "Wow."

"You say that a lot."

"I mean it. How did this happen?"

"Did I mention that Alex is the shit? I mean he's big business, or at least he used to be when he was here. His name still brings fear to a lot of people. If you want, we can eat out."

Millie scrunched up her face. "I'm kind of tired. Can we just stay here, eat, talk, and relax?"

"You're a girl after my own heart."

"Ah, it doesn't take much."

"It never usually does." He winked at her.

A warm fuzzy feeling wrapped around Millie's heart. She loved being with Baker. Leaving him had been so hard for her, but again, she couldn't do it. She couldn't bring herself to love a man who still loved his wife. Brian had taught her a lot about what she actually wanted out of life. Talking about her family, it only served to remind her exactly what she wanted. She wanted a love like her grandparents'.

Staring at Baker, she wondered if he truly was the one.

Chapter Six

Lash sat at the bar, sipping on his coffee, and staring at the figures in front of him. The gym was running at a profit, which was good. Last year when they finally opened it, the losses had been huge. Now, they were becoming comfortable again, which for him was a relief. Looking through the figures, all of their businesses were turning profits. The warehouse they owned outside of Fort Wills was still just a training ground for them. They had so many different ideas for it, but Lash just wasn't sure. He liked it to still be their safe house. There had been many changes, and modifications along the way. Even after three years of no bad shit, he wasn't willing to give up a potential place that could save their damn lives.

"Guess what I found," Whizz said, dropping a file onto the mountain that Lash already had to go through.

"You're a girl, and Lacey's bi," Lash said.

"Ha, ha, very funny. Nope, what I found out is that our girl Millie could be due to inherit a shitload of cash."

"So? Baker asked you not to dig."

"My curious brain made me."

Lash looked over the figures he was looking at. "You're going to try and justify your snooping?"

"Yep, every single hacker does. Anyway, I got into her background. Her family is a piece of work. I'm shocked she's even remotely nice."

"How can you even make an assessment on someone by just looking at a bunch of facts and figures?"

"Hello, master hacker here. I don't just look at all random files or databases. I also do a mass check on all social media. Let's just say her family is not well liked."

Whizz shrugged. "Grandma likes Millie though. Woman knows her security. She made it a little tough for me to get into her system, but I got it. It would seem that in the event of Grandma passing, the entire Levy fortune, in the town where she lives, that's big news, everything will go to Millie. Bypasses everyone, and goes to the youngest daughter. Do you think Baker knows?"

"I think if he wants to know everything about Millie, he'll ask. He didn't want this," Lash said, pointing at the file.

"I know. I just like to know everything about everyone. Oh, your latest health checkup is clean."

"Why the fuck are you looking at my medical records?" Lash asked.

"I was curious, and seeing as you're my Prez, I wanted to make sure you're in the peak of health."

"Whizz—"

"I'm a darling, I know. I started checking everyone's when Sally became a regular visitor. I like to make sure my girl is looked after. Also, Lacey's latest checkup was fine, no cause for concern. I worry about it. You know with all the possible cancer scares, and everything that can go wrong with a woman's body. Vagina and tits aside, I'm scared."

"I don't even want to think about shit that may never happen," Lash said. He didn't want to think of all the potential health crap that could happen to his girl, and that he couldn't fight.

"Speaking of, have you told her about your planned vasectomy?" Whizz asked.

Lash stared at his friend. Whizz had been through a lot. A great deal more than a lot of the brothers. He'd been taken by Alan, one of their former enemies, who was now dead. Raped, beaten, tortured, and on the brink of death. The only person strong enough to help Whizz had been Lacey.

"You shouldn't go nosing around in other people's business, Whizz."

"I know, but seeing as Angel is one of the sweetest women I know, and I happened to find that, I was curious about how much you've told her."

Glaring at Whizz, Lash put all the files down.

"She has a right to know," Whizz said. "I've heard her talking about more kids. She doesn't want to stop at Anthony and Chloe, and seeing as you're the other half of their DNA, you need to tell her, Prez." Whizz smiled, and rubbed his hands together. "That will be all from me today."

"I almost lost her."

"What?"

"Our first kid, she lost through an attack. She tried to kill herself, and I almost lost her twice with one kid. Anthony came along, and it was a difficult pregnancy. Then what happened with Chloe. Some couples are only supposed to have a couple of kids. Angel and I, we've got our two kids, and I'm not willing to risk her life for anymore."

"It's not just your decision, brother." Whizz didn't say anything more about that. "Oh, I also found an updated version of Grandma's will. It would seem Millie's Grandma may decide to sell the business. From what I gather, the son, Millie's father, is not to be trusted, and he's been trying to hide funds into a secured bank account. No one else knows of her plans."

"Who does the money go to in the event of a sale?" Lash asked.

"Millie, on Grandma's deathbed. The Grandma is kickass secretive. The reason she has been in Italy for a while now, besides the beauty and the air, she's been having secret business meetings away from the board.

She, and she alone, has the power to sell. I don't know what this means to Millie, but I'd say a couple of Levys won't be too happy about having their livelihood taken away." He walked away.

Lash hadn't thought about the vasectomy appointment he'd made. It was weeks ago, and he had another month until he went for the operation. Talking to Angel about it just never seemed like the right time.

"Hey," Murphy said, taking a seat. "You got time to talk?"

"It seems I don't have much of a choice." The files of paperwork were going to have to wait. Was this what Tiny had to put up with all the time? "What can I do for you?"

"Tate."

"Ugh! What has she done now?" Lash rubbed at his temple, really not in the mood to deal with her shit. After his parents died, he and Nash had to grow up with her. Of course, Tate wasn't always such a bitch. That little surprise in her personality came later in life.

"She has given me the opportunity to move."

"To move? Like house?"

"Like house, like location, like job."

Lash froze. "That's new."

"Yeah. I don't know if this is a hint that she wants to leave, or she thinks that I want to leave. Either way, I don't want to make the wrong decision."

"What did she say?" Lash asked. Ten minutes later, Lash blew out a breath. "This is a decision for you. Tate is giving you the choice here, brother. I don't think this is a deal-breaker in your relationship. The club doesn't have to be your life."

"I wanted it to be."

"Times change, people change. We all do. This is the choice you're going to have to make, and then you're going to have to bring it to church."

"Fuck, I was hoping you'd tell me to give Tate some flowers, and love her a little."

"Yeah, this is a couple choice that you need to make as a couple."

"Fort Wills is our home."

"Do what you want to do, and what feels right to you. Right now, I really need to deal with this." He pointed at the files.

"Oh, yeah, sorry."

"Talk with Tate. Really talk. If you want, Angel and I will take Simon and Isabella. You can have a nice long evening and night with your woman."

"Thanks, Lash. I'll take you up on that soon."

Lash watched Murphy walk away.

Picking up the stack of files once again, Lash flicked them open.

"Hey, brother," Nash said, taking a seat.

"What the fuck now?"

Nash held his hands up. "What the fuck?"

"What do you want? Some magical wand to make your dick big? What?"

"I was just going to sit with you and drink coffee. Right now, I think I'll go elsewhere."

Gritting his teeth, Lash watched his brother walk away. Picking up the large file of documents, he headed into the office, and stopped when he saw Tiny.

"Are you struggling?" Tiny asked.

"No one will leave me alone long enough to deal with this shit. It's not like good stuff they're coming to me with either. Tate's thinking of moving, or at least has given Murphy the option to pursue whatever he wants, Whizz is on my back about shit. Nash just wants to hang out."

Tiny held up his hand. "What's the problem?"

"I don't have time for petty shit."

"This club is more than a bunch of men shooting the shit, Lash. This is a family."

"Yeah, and guess what? Families deal with their shit."

"Actually, they all help each other out. It's not about sending one off to do other stuff, while another moans about it." Tiny folded his arms, staring at him. He pointed at the files. "The good thing about that shit in your hands, it'll be there tomorrow, in a week, in a fucking month, and you'll always have time to deal with it. Whizz deals with your first point of defense. That computer crap he does, it's his battleground, and he's got us out of some sticky fucking messes. Murphy, he's my son-in-law. You don't understand what is going on there, and my daughter is far away from Fort Wills. Murphy is a good and loyal brother. Why does he want to leave?"

"I don't know, Tate offered."

"Yeah, why did she offer? What the hell is going on in their life that they need to move? This is your club, Lash. Your family. You came to me whenever a problem happened with Angel, remember. When she was in that psych ward, and you didn't know what to do, who did you come to?"

"I came to you, and you fixed it."

"I got you talking to the doctor. I put you on the path of understanding what was wrong with your woman. I didn't need to do that, Lash. She was your woman, your problem, you could fix it. The reason The Skulls work, and work well, is because we're more than a bunch of men shooting the shit. We're a family. We work together. It's what keeps us strong."

Lash nodded. "Fuck, I'm sorry. I just, I don't want to fail."

"You won't fail. I won't let you, and neither will

any of them out there."

"Don't you want to take the club back? I'd gladly have you back in charge."

"Not a chance, son. This is your life now, and you're doing so damn good. I'm proud of you."

****

After settling for grilled cheese themselves, Baker and Millie stared out of the penthouse window, watching the passing city go by.

"I could never live here all the time. Look how crazy it is," she said.

"This is the main strip. I imagine further away, it's easier to deal with."

"Still couldn't live here. So many different vices to cave to. Drink, drugs, sex, gambling, not to mention the all you can eat buffets that are available."

He chuckled. "You'd sit eating all day?"

"Sometimes I think I could. Start from one end, and work my way through the entire table."

Baker gripped her shoulders, staring out. "You couldn't even eat four grilled cheese sandwiches. I think you're safe from eating so much." He pressed a kiss to her neck.

"I love it when you do that."

He'd seen her nipples grow hard every time he kissed or touched her neck. Leaning down, he flicked his tongue over her pulse before sucking on the spot. She moaned, leaning back against him.

"It's an erogenous zone. It would be so hard to resist me." Moving his hands to her waist, he slowly started to slide them up. "There are many parts of your body that would make it hard to resist me." Just beneath her breasts, he stopped.

Her breathing was heavy. "You're just going to tease me, aren't you?"

"Teasing is a good thing. I'll drive you crazy until you're begging me."

Running his hands down her body, he cupped her hips, giving them a squeeze. He couldn't keep his hands to himself. It was next to impossible to do.

Sucking on her neck again, he forced himself to pull away.

"Why did you stop?" she asked, turning toward him.

"Because I'm not going to be the bad guy here. I want to touch you, but you've not given me permission to."

She smiled, and damn it made his stomach tighten. What was this woman doing to him? Since he'd been able to finally say goodbye to Katie, it was like a weight had been lifted off his shoulders, and now staring at Millie, she was the sunshine to him. The bright light.

"I give permission because I'm not pushing you away. I like your hands on my body. I don't want you to stop."

"You don't?"

"Well, I don't want to go all the way. I'm not ready."

"That I understand."

She stepped up to him, placing her hands on his chest. "I'm going to go and take a shower." Millie went on her tiptoes, and kissed his lips. "Don't go anywhere."

"I won't."

He watched her disappear into the bedroom. The bathroom was through to the en-suite. His cock was so damn hard, and he wanted her. He wouldn't spoil their time together though. This was about them getting to know each other without all the crap with it.

"Keep your shit together, Baker."

His cell phone started to ring, and flicking it

open, he saw it was Alex.

"Hello, miss me already?" Baker asked.

"Ha-ha. I just wanted to make sure you got there safely. Butch gave me a call, but it has been some time since I was last there. Is everything good?"

"Everything looks good. The fridge is fully stocked, which was a surprise."

"You wanted a week away. You don't even have to leave the penthouse if you don't want to. If you do, the casino has everything you could want. Playing, gambling, partying, and there's a good restaurant."

"You thought of everything."

"Of course. It's what a good manager does. I think of absolutely everything."

In the background he heard a baby whimper.

"Shoot, I've got to go. We'll be heading out on Monday I think. We'll meet up, have some dinner."

"Sure."

They said their goodbyes, and Baker hung up the phone.

Moving into the bedroom, he saw the bathroom door was partially open. The sound of water running became the biggest temptation in his life.

No, don't do it.

Do it. Go and see.

Baker stepped forward, then stepped back. Two steps forward, one step back. Each time he got just a little bit closer than the last time before until he was stood at the doorway.

Millie was humming to herself.

She's all alone.

She's completely naked, soaking wet, and all alone.

You could give her some company.

Baker removed his jacket and threw it onto the

bed. Taking his shirt off, he dropped it to the floor, and entered the bathroom. The frosted glass of the shower didn't help him get a clear view of Millie's naked body. His jeans were on the floor in the next second, and he couldn't wait.

Millie belonged to him, and there was never going to be another man in her life. He accepted that, and knew without a doubt he would work his ass off to keep her.

Opening the shower door, he heard her scream.

"It's just me."

"Baker, what the hell? I'm naked."

"So, it's not like I've not seen it before."

"Not from me, you haven't. Okay, you've seen a little bit, but come on."

"Millie, you and I, it's happening. We both know it's going to happen. There's no denying it. I'm not going to force you, but, however, I'm going to get you used to me."

She presented her back and turned her head. "I'm … crap, you're huge." She quickly faced the front. "I'm so sorry. I shouldn't have looked."

He couldn't hold back his laughter anymore. "I want your eyes on me. I'd love your hands, too." Reaching past her head, he grabbed the soap, rubbing the lavender scent into his hands. Placing it back on the little tray, he put his hands on her hips.

She jumped, letting out a little squeal. "I wasn't ready."

Pulling her back against him, he cupped her tits. "You've got to learn to trust me, babe."

"I do."

"Really? Right now, it doesn't feel like it. We're here together. To make this work. Do you want to, or should we head back home?"

"No. I want to make it work."

"Then let me touch. Let me look."

"No one has ever seen me like this."

"Your ex was a fucking loser." He spun her around so she had no choice but to look at him. Taking her hand, he placed it around his dick. "Do you know what you're doing to me? This doesn't happen for anyone. I want you. I want you so damn bad that I can taste it. Every time I'm with you, you make me hard. This doesn't happen for just anyone. Only you."

She stared at his cock, and her hand started to move up and down the length, pumping him little by little.

"I've never, I didn't know."

"You know now. This is what you do to me. All the time." Wrapping his fingers around hers, he showed her exactly what he liked and exactly how he liked it. He released a moan. "Yeah, baby, exactly like that." Squeezing his fingers, he made her do it just a little bit tighter.

"Isn't that hurting you?"

"No, it feels so good. I don't want you to stop. I'm going to touch you, Millie. Please, let me." He let go of her hand around his cock, allowing her to do what she wanted. Her hand on him was all he wanted anyway.

"Yes."

Putting his hands on her hips, he started to work them up to cup her tits. They were so big, more than a generous handful with tight, red nipples. At the moment those nipples were rock hard letting him know how aroused she actually was.

"I love your tits, Millie. So big and ripe." He leaned forward and claimed one of her nipples, sucking it into his mouth. Baker lifted both of her breasts up as if to make an offering to himself. Biting down on her nipple, he flicked the bud to soothe the sting he'd created.

She moaned, arching up for more.

"You want me to suck on these beauties?"

"Yes."

Releasing her tits, he stepped back. "Then offer them to me."

"What?"

"Offer me your tits. We've got all the time in the world. No one is waiting for us. Offer those tits to me, Millie."

She hesitated for a split second, and during that short time, he thought he'd fucked up. Then her hands moved beneath her breasts, and she lifted up on her tiptoes.

"What do you want me to do?"

"Suck them please."

"You want me to suck on your titties?"

"Yes."

"Say it then, Millie. Tell me what you want. Talk dirty to me."

Her cheeks were a beautiful shade of red. Not once did she demand that he stop.

"Suck on my titties, Baker, please."

"Always so polite. Do you like me talking dirty to you?"

"Yes, I do."

Stepping forward, he gripped her ass, tugged her close, and sucked one of the beaded nipples into his mouth. Water ran all over them. Baker didn't care. His hands were full of a beautiful woman. A beautiful woman that had been driving him crazy for a long time, and one he intended to keep for the rest of his life.

Millie Levy was his, and he knew without a doubt he was in love with her.

This kind, beautiful woman, had the power to

ease his soul, and to grant him the gift of loving again. He wasn't ever going to let her go.

****

Biting her lip, Millie fisted her hands at her side, not knowing what to do. Baker's lips on her breasts felt so good, so right.

"Touch me, Millie," Baker said. He took her hands, placing them on his body. He was the complete opposite of her. She was soft whereas he was rock hard.

Opening her hands, she ran them down his back, and then up again, sinking them into his hair. She closed her eyes, letting out a little gasp as he bit her nipple hard. The pain disappeared as his tongue danced over the pain, sending shockwaves of pleasure rushing through her.

"You taste so good." Suddenly, he was gone, and she stared down to see him kneeling before her.

"Baker, what are you doing?"

His fingers circled her ankle. "There's more of you to taste." His gaze went to her pussy. "And I'd really like a taste."

She'd never been one to go bare on her pussy. Millie kept it nice and trimmed as she didn't like it to be too big and thick.

Damn, she was thinking about keeping her womanly bits in check, and Baker was on his knees staring at her pussy and licking his lips. It was like her fantasy had come to life, and she didn't have a clue what to do, or how to handle everything.

"Baker?"

"Trust me. I can make you feel so good."

He *was* making her feel so good.

"I trust you."

Baker lifted her foot, and she closed her eyes, not knowing what else to do.

"Look at that pretty little pussy. It's begging for

my cock, Millie."

"How do you know?"

"Because I know what it wants, and I know what I want. For now, it'll have to make do with my mouth."

She bit her lip as he placed her foot on the lip on the side of the shower.

"I have to wonder if Alex designed this shower for this purpose."

Millie opened her eyes then, and saw that the little foot rest was in the perfect place for a woman to be open to a man.

Baker stared into her eyes as he closed the distance, taking her clit into his mouth and sucking it. The moment he touched her, Millie lost all sound thought. It was amazing. His mouth, his tongue as it glided over her clit—she'd never felt anything so magical. It was even better than his fingers.

He sucked her clit into his mouth, using his teeth to gnaw a little. She loved the pain and pleasure combined. Both sensations were almost too much for her, and yet at the same time not enough.

His hands moved to grab her ass, and spread her cheeks open. "I'm going to claim every single part of you. Your pussy, your mouth, and your ass. Not a part of you won't know who I am."

"Baker?" She didn't know why she spoke his name.

"It's okay, baby. I'll prepare you. I'll always prepare you for everything. You'll want for nothing. All you've got to do is give yourself to me."

She let out a yelp as his finger slid down the crack of her ass. He simply applied a little pressure to her anus, and even that created a sensation she wasn't entirely sure of.

"Don't worry. By the time I take you there, you'll

be screaming and begging for me to take you."

He spoke a lot about begging. Was he used to women begging for him, wanting him? Millie closed down those thoughts. Baker wasn't that kind of man. If she knew something about him, he wasn't the kind to go screwing random strangers, or was he?

Baker sucked her clit into his mouth at the same time that he teased her anus. Both sensations distracted her enough to stop thinking about the other women in his life. They didn't matter. Nothing actually mattered but the two of them in this moment.

"So tasty. I could spend all night and all day, licking you."

As nice as that sounded, she didn't think she could handle that kind of attention all day. Her stomach started to tighten as Baker repeatedly flicked her clit, teasing her. He didn't stop, and he pressed against her ass at the same time. The dual sensation was more than she could stand.

She screamed his name as her orgasm washed over in such a rush that she almost fell on her ass if Baker hadn't caught her, holding her steady.

He didn't stop. He continued to tease, suck, and stroke her clit until she had no choice but to beg him to stop.

It was all too much.

Finally, after what felt like a lifetime, he pressed a kiss to her clit, and sat back. She stared into his eyes, blue, like the ocean, and fell hard.

"You're so beautiful when you let go," he said, licking his lips.

Heat filled her cheeks, and she glanced down to see his cock was still rock hard. "Do you want me to take care of that?" she asked.

"Do you think you're ready for that?"

"I'd like to give you exactly what you gave me."

He got to his feet and touched her cheek. "You're always surprising me." He tilted her head back, sliding his tongue across her lips, she opened up. Meeting him halfway, she slid her tongue across his.

"I'm ready to learn."

Enough time had passed, and she saw the change inside Baker. It wasn't an instant change. It had taken him years to be the man he now was.

"The things you do to me." He growled, biting her lip as he did.

Sinking down to her knees, she stared up at him. "What do you want to do?"

"You do know that this is every single guy's desire. To have a woman at their feet ready to service them."

"I'm not interested in servicing anyone. I'm here for you, Baker." Running her hands up and down his thighs, she smiled. "Only you."

"Wrap your hands around my cock."

The way he ordered her made her even wetter, even if that was possible. She'd only just experienced her release. Was it possible for her to be ready to have another? Damn, she had been missing so much.

She held his cock and stared at the tip, which was leaking pre-cum.

"Lick it, baby."

Millie licked the tip, moaning as she tasted him for the first time.

"Now take me into your mouth, and suck it."

She covered the tip, and sucked him into her mouth. He let out a groan, and she looked up in time to see his eyes roll back in his head.

Releasing him, she frowned. "Are you okay?"

"It feels so good, don't stop."

Sucking his cock into her mouth, she closed her eyes, enjoying everything she was doing.

Bobbing her head, she took him to the back of her throat, pulling back up. With each dip of her head, she took him even further into her mouth, avoiding the need to gag.

"Fuck, Millie, that feels so fucking good." He started to thrust his hips. When his hands caught her head, she opened her eyes, and stared up to find him watching. "So good. Take my cock, baby."

She held onto his thighs, as he used her mouth for his pleasure.

He fucked her mouth, and she couldn't look away. Seeing how much he was enjoying her attentions turned her on, and she didn't want to stop.

"Oh fuck!" Baker pulled out, and she gasped as the tip exploded, shooting white drops onto her breasts. His orgasm went on and on, spraying her as he did. Baker sank down to his knees, kissing her. His hands went into her hair, and this was different. She didn't know why, but it just felt completely different. "Thank you."

"What for?"

"For waiting for me. For not giving up."

"I walked away from you, Baker."

"You didn't move on though. You could have been with someone else, and yet you weren't. You were with me the whole way."

She touched his face. "You made me dirty." Having that date with Jack, it was the first one she'd ever been on since being in Fort Wills. She'd explained her past to Baker, and because of Bethany, her sister, she'd withdrawn from dating, believing she was unlovable.

"I'll clean you." He kissed her lips and helped her to feet.

Baker spun her to face the showerhead, grabbing the soap, and began to massage his scented hands into her skin. Leaning against him, she closed her eyes. "I don't want this to end."

"It won't." He nuzzled her neck, and the shower lasted for a lot longer. They touched, washed, and simply basked in the time together. Nothing was interrupting their time, and Millie found that she didn't want to break their bubble, which was exactly what was going on.

When there was no reason to stay in the shower, Baker turned it off, grabbing a towel. She watched as he wrapped a towel around his waist, and then turned to her with another. "Come on, baby."

Walking into his arms, she took the towel from him, and started to dry her body.

Words didn't seem necessary as they got dressed. When she made to get a nightshirt, he placed a hand on her arm. "You don't need to cover up for me. Tonight I want to hold you."

She always wore something to bed. Baker threw his towel into the bathroom, and he climbed into the bed, tapping the bed. "Come on, baby."

"Oh, er, I've never slept naked."

"Never?"

"No, never."

"Come on. It'll be another first, Millie. Come and enjoy."

Staring at the nightshirts, she closed the drawer, and made her way toward the bed. He pulled the sheets back, and she climbed inside, staring up at the ceiling. "It's a day of firsts for me."

"This is going to be an entire lifetime of firsts."

She turned toward him. Baker was lying on his side with his head resting on his hands. Rolling over to face him, she placed her hand on his chest. "Tell me about your wife."

He didn't tense up, or change the subject. "She was the most beautiful girl I'd ever seen." He smiled. "We were friends as kids, and it changed as we grew up."

"The love changed?"

"Yeah, I fancied her like crazy. Had a big crush on her, and I knew I was going to marry her."

"Does it hurt?"

"No, not anymore. What happened, happened. I can't change that."

"Would you change that?" she asked, wondering if she should be pushing it.

"Once I thought I would, but then this wouldn't have happened?"

"What?"

"Us. I wouldn't have ever met you, and I wouldn't be with The Skulls. I never thought I'd say this after she was taken from me, but I actually like my life, Millie, and I wouldn't trade you for the world."

It had to be the nicest thing anyone had ever said to her.

Chapter Seven

"So what do you want to do? Poker tables, slot machines, cards, maybe even some dancing?" Baker asked, putting his arms in the air, and giving a shake of his hips. He got the desired effect. Millie burst out laughing.

"I like the idea of dancing." She then proceeded to throw her hands in the air and shake her ass.

"Oh, now those moves are perfection." He grabbed her hips, and in the center of the casino, he ground against her. "See, we've got the hang of this. Do you want to par-tay?"

She giggled, spinning around, and wrapping her arms around his neck. "I promised myself when I came here, that I would pick one slot machine, and place one coin inside." She held up one single coin. "Would you like to play one game of chance?"

"I'll be anywhere with you. However, I think you're going to need more than one coin."

"So? I know loads of people just throw good money after bad into those machines, and the truth is, the machine will only ever pay out after a coin, or when it's ready. What do you say?"

He grabbed his own coin, and held it up. "Two coins, for two different people. We do it together. Two different machines."

"That is what I'm talking about."

They changed their coins for the relevant chips, and then started looking at the slot machines. Baker figured she'd just pick any random machine, but not Millie. She stared at each one.

"Does it really matter which machine you use?"

"Probably not, but it's my money, and I want to

spend it wisely."

She moved down the long aisles. Every now and then she'd stop, watching as people plowed chips into the machine. He saw one woman had nearly five hundred dollars' worth of chips. Alex did tell him that a casino was a legal way of earning dough, and taking it from someone else. Gambling, the addiction, was an awful situation.

Baker had seen many people fight it, and very few overcome it.

"I don't think it really matters, sweetie. Your money is going to lose no matter what."

"You're killing my buzz, Baker. Come on, live a little."

"I have a hundred dollars and some more for you to blow, and you're blowing one coin."

Millie looked back at him. "Then consider me a cheap date. Found it."

She stepped forward, and pushed the chip inside the machine. She pulled the lever, and waited.

Nothing happened.

"Right, here it goes." Baker placed his chip inside, pulled the lever, and … he won the jackpot. Alarms and celebration started sounding. "Holy shit."

Millie giggled, and for the next thirty minutes, it was kind of surreal. With his woman at his side, he took the check worth ten thousand dollars, and declined their best room. Finally, when all the fuss had gone, and he pocketed the real check, with the large one being sent to his room, Baker wrapped his arms around her. "You still needed two chips."

"But only one chip to win, baby," she said. "It didn't matter what I put in first. It's only what you put in."

Baker wrapped his arms around her. "Come on,

let's go dancing."

He spun her around, and someone had been close to them. Millie bumped into them. "Oh, I'm so sorry," she said.

The man turned around with a frown on his face. "Millie."

She stepped back, going into Baker's arms. "Brian."

This was the asshole ex.

Baker couldn't help but glare at the bastard. Wow, talk about coincidence.

Why glare? You won. She's in your arms, and no one is going to steal her away.

Wrapping his arm around her waist, Baker stared at her ex, waiting for shit to go down.

"I've not seen you in years. Not since you ran out on me at the church. You know you made me look like an idiot." Brain folded his arms and glared at her. "Do you know how stupid I looked?"

Millie tensed up, and Baker was about to interrupt when his woman exploded.

"Are you for real? I humiliated *you*? You have no right to blame me. As it happens, on *my* wedding day, I saw you screwing *my sister*. Yeah, I saw the two of you, and I heard you. You couldn't even stand to be near me. Don't you dare try to make out that I was the one in the wrong. *You* were in the wrong, and you should never have proposed to me. You should have married Bethany."

"She wouldn't have me. You don't think I tried. She only wants to fuck, and well, she was bad for my image."

Millie flinched. "Oh, so you went for me so that you could be closer to her?"

"No. Bethany was the one that came on to me.

Once *we* didn't get married, I was more than willing to marry her, and she laughed at me. Your sister, she's a fucking bitch, and I'm sorry."

"Did it stop you from sleeping with her?" Millie asked.

"No. Why are you here?" he asked. "I thought you were against gambling."

"I'm having fun. What the hell are you doing here?"

Brian nodded toward a group of men. "I'm here on a bachelor party. I still see Bethany from time to time."

"Good for you." Shaking her head, she turned toward Baker. "I want to go and dance."

"You're a loser. I can't believe you didn't see a good thing when you had it," Baker said. "Your loss is my gain."

Moving her toward the nightclub within the casino, he took her to the bar, and ordered them both shots.

"I don't drink."

"I'd say you really need to have a drink."

"Ugh, I hate him. I hate that I've just had to do that." She ran her fingers through her hair. "From one high to a complete low."

"You never said that you ran out without them realizing it."

"Didn't I? I thought it went without saying."

"No. I figured you canceled the wedding and gave some notice to everyone."

Millie shook her head. "All I wanted to do was get out of there, and get out of there fast. He was screwing my sister."

"You didn't humiliate him enough as far as I'm concerned."

"No? What would you have had me do?"

"Simple. When it came time to say I do, say 'I don't, you lying, cheating bastard', and then turn to your sister, bitch slap her, and leave."

Millie laughed. "I should have, shouldn't I? According to my grandma, I was enemy number one. I made a lot of people look bad, and I wasn't even trying. I just wanted to get far away from all the crazy stuff."

The barman placed a couple of shots in front of them. "Drink. You deserve it."

"I'm going to be a lightweight. I feel I should warn you."

"Don't worry. I'll drink enough for the two of us." He took one shot, swallowing it down in one gulp. "Damn, that's good."

Millie swallowed it down, coughed, and wheezed. "Wow, that is so strong."

"Good, isn't it?"

"I don't know. Let's go dancing before I can't feel my feet."

"One shot won't do that to you?"

"I'm a lightweight, remember, and I'm not afraid to admit that."

They made their way onto the dance floor. Millie wrapped her arms around him, and together, they danced to the fast beat of the music.

To Baker, everything faded away until they were the only two people alive in the world.

When the music changed to a slow number, he didn't let her go, nor did Millie release him.

"I like this," she said, whispering the words against his ear.

"I know. I like it as well."

She snuggled against him. "I never thought I could be happy, Baker. Thank you for proving that I can."

He kissed the top of her head, knowing in his heart that he'd do anything to keep that smile on her face.

They danced late into the night until Millie complained of sore feet, even in her sneakers.

Baker took her up to their room, and helped her out of her clothes, and into bed.

"No sexy shower time today?"

"You're not ready for a sexy shower time." He'd given her two more shots, and she was buzzing.

She was so adorable after a little drink.

"My head is spinning a little bit. Is that normal?"

"Not on three shots, but seeing as it's your first, we'll make an exception."

"I love being here with you. I was so nervous about coming away with you. I was scared about going on a date. I just want to be loved for me, you know."

"I know."

"You were always so sad. Like all the time. I'd see you staring at your ring. It wouldn't be obvious or in front of me. You were parked across the road from the shop once, and I was going to come and say hi to you. You stared at the shop. I don't think you saw me. I waved, but you didn't wave back. Then you stared down at your ring, and you shook your head. I knew. You weren't ready. You love your wife, and I guess I was a little jealous as well. She was really something. I want to be that something to a man. Where the thought of losing me makes him grieve."

"I wonder if you'll remember this in the morning."

"I hope so. I never thought you'd come and say hi to me, or not wear your ring. The moment I saw your hand bare, I just knew. I knew I didn't want to wait anymore. I wanted you to give us a chance."

"We waited long enough."

"We did, and I like that." She reached out, touching his cheek. "You're so good to me."

Her eyes closed, falling to sleep. "You're such an adorable drunk." He dropped a kiss to her lips.

After checking that the penthouse was secured for the night, he followed her to bed, stripping down naked, and joining her.

****

Millie rolled over and winced. Her head was pounding, and her mouth tasted funny.

"Hello, my little partier."

"Ugh." She opened one eye, and then the other. Baker was stood holding out a glass of water, and some pills. "Are those magic pills?"

"Depends? They cure all headaches."

"Then they are magic." She sat up in bed, moaning. "I only had like three shots. This is ridiculous."

"Why? It's not unheard of. So you got into a little partying mood last night. It happens."

"Not to me it doesn't." She drank the entire glass of water. "I'm not good at the whole handling my alcohol."

Baker sat on the edge of the bed as she lay back, wondering if the pain would ever cease.

"Some people handle alcohol differently."

"What about you? Any headache?"

"Nope. Nothing. Just needed to take a really long leak this morning."

She wrinkled her nose. "Next time, no shots."

"You had fun, didn't you?"

"I did."

"Any blank spots about last night?"

"Nope. I remember everything. Bumping into Brian, and him trying to accuse me of humiliating him. I hate him even more. I also remember telling you about the time I saw you waiting outside my shop. Your wife. I hoped I didn't hurt you."

"No, you didn't."

Millie tucked some of her matted hair behind her ear. "Can I ask you something?"

"Sure."

"What changed?"

"What do you mean?"

"Well, one moment you were staring at your ring, and looking like you never wanted to let it go, and then you were wanting to date me, and ready for us to come away together. Love like you had with Katie, it doesn't stop."

"It didn't stop. The pain, it faded away, and my acceptance of it took some time. It hasn't been overnight, Millie. I've been dealing for over five years now. I think that's long enough to finally put to bed the demons of my past."

"Was it demonic?"

"It was a hard time. I never thought I'd find love again."

Her heart skipped a little beat. "Do you think differently?"

"I do. I think love is possible if you're ready for it. What about you?"

"I don't know if love exists for everyone. I've not been lucky enough to find it."

"Maybe someone will surprise you when you least expect it."

She stared into his blue eyes, wondering. "Yeah, maybe they will."

Baker gripped her thigh. "Just so you know, Alex and Sunshine are heading in tonight."

"Will they be staying here?"

"Nope. They're staying with Cheryl and Butch."

"Interesting."

"It'll certainly be drama, or maybe not. Distance has made the heart grow fonder. Also, Butch is downstairs with Cheryl. How do you feel about a spot of breakfast?"

Millie nodded, then moaned.

"Maybe not?" Baker asked.

"No, no, I want to go. I don't want any excuse to stay in bed, and cry over the fact I've got a hangover. It has to be in some special record. Girl gets hung-over with three shots."

"I think Sally could do better than you."

Millie blew a raspberry. "I'll be ready in ten minutes."

Thirty minutes later they were heading downstairs. Millie's hair just wouldn't go, and her stomach kept turning. She refused to be sick, even though there was no way she'd be able to control it.

Coffee, food, and time, and she hoped she'd be back to being sprightly.

Butch and Cheryl were sitting at a table together, laughing.

Both of them turned, and Millie pasted a smile onto her face.

"Hey," Baker said.

"Sorry we're late. I couldn't get my hair to go right. I had a little too much to drink last night," Millie said, sliding in.

She caught Baker rolling his eyes. "By too much to drink, she means three shots."

"That's a lightweight," Cheryl said.

"I know. I don't drink, like ever. I know why now."

"Hi, I'm Cheryl. We've not been properly

introduced."

They shook hands.

"Where's Michael?"

"He's with Ned, training," Cheryl said. "He likes to fight, and he's having a few problems with his anger. Ned promised to help channel that anger."

"He'll do it, babe," Butch said.

"I'm hoping Alex can help out."

Millie saw a look pass between Butch and Cheryl that clearly went a little deeper than an anger-riddled kid.

A waiter came to the table, and Millie ordered a really strong espresso. Baker ordered them toast, scrambled eggs, and bacon. Her stomach growled.

"I'm so sorry. I really don't know what is wrong with me today," she said. Her cheeks were on fire.

"It's nice of you to come out to Vegas," Cheryl said.

"It was a last minute thing. I wanted time alone with my girl here, and Vegas was all I could think of."

"You can get married here," Butch said. "Very easily done."

"Oh, we're not here to get married. We just want to spend some time getting to know each other," Millie said.

She wasn't ready for marriage. At least, not yet. She'd already been screwed over by her first attempt, and she didn't even make it to the altar.

"So, how are you?" Baker asked.

"We're good. We're expecting," Butch said, kissing Cheryl's neck.

"Really? How far along?" Millie asked. She did love kids. It was one of the reasons she loved owning a toy shop.

Seeing the magic in their eyes when they discovered something new, she loved to watch.

"Only a couple of months," Cheryl said. "We didn't want to announce it."

"We've had some difficulty conceiving."

"Oh, I'm so sorry." Millie patted Cheryl's hand, trying to offer her comfort.

"How come the club doesn't know about this?" Baker asked.

"Baker, you and I both know that this is not a club situation. I got sent out here as part of my punishment." Butch held his hands up. "I respected the decision, and I wouldn't change it. Even though it has been difficult, and a struggle. We've been able to make a life here, and it's a good life."

"There has been some difficulty though," Cheryl said. "He does get homesick, and so does Michael. I think he misses his father a lot. I know I miss Fort Wills. Vegas is a great place. It's always busy."

"That's the problem, right?" Millie asked. "It's always busy. Always something going on."

"Ned runs in some bad circles, and some of the guys he has fighting are pretty scary." Cheryl looked a little pale. "It has been an adjustment."

Millie stared at the couple. They were clearly in love, and were fighting whatever problems they faced together.

Their breakfasts came, and Millie dived in, moaning at the fluffy scrambled eggs and crispy bacon. She was so hungry.

Baker and Butch kept on talking. She enjoyed listening to the easy banter between the two men.

Cheryl looked a little sick, and when she made a mad dash toward the bathroom, Millie excused herself to follow the other woman.

"Are you okay?" Millie asked.

It was one of the rare occasions the bathroom was

in fact empty.

"Yeah, it's morning sickness. It comes and goes, you know."

Cheryl exited the cubicle, wiping her mouth with some of the tissue.

"I want this kid so bad, you know?"

"I don't have children, but I can imagine. Have you been trying long?"

"Over five years. At first when we moved out here, neither of us wanted any kids. Vegas was different from everything I'd known, and even from what Butch had known. Ned is a great guy. He's the kind of guy you don't cross, and providing you don't, you'll always be on his good side."

"I think I understand."

"He's a one man army. Honestly, you say his name, and people are scared. Seeing the men he deals with, it can all just be a little too much at times." Cheryl washed her face. "I've lost three babies in the past."

"I'm so sorry."

"It's not your fault. It just wasn't meant to be." Cheryl dried her face. "Come on, let's go out to the others."

****

Sally sat on the couch at her home. Daisy had already gone to bed while Lacey and Whizz had gone out for the night. She'd offered to look after her little sister. Her study books lay at the side of her, and she just couldn't bring herself to pick them up. Ever since Steven had sprung that question upon her a few days ago, she'd been struggling to deal with anything else.

Why did he have to ask that kind of question now? She didn't get it. Standing up, she waited to make sure that her leg was fine. After a long day of walking around, she was always careful about her leg. The prosthetic she'd gotten was brilliant. However, the human body was not perfect, and there were times she just couldn't bring herself to stand upright.

Going away to college was supposed to be about her finding her independence, and her place in the world. All it had done was make her homesick, wishing she hadn't gone away. She had held off for a year before heading off to college. She'd been nineteen when she started, and now two years later, she still wasn't getting anything from the experience. Drew was a great support, but again, he wasn't home. He wasn't family.

Entering the kitchen, she grabbed everything to make a hot chocolate. In The Skulls, it was Angel's drink of choice to help everyone to feel better. She adored Angel. Sally found Angel calming. Even when she was stressed, Angel always seemed to know what to say and do to take that worry away. She was like an angel. Lacey didn't mind. Sally adored her mother, Lacey.

Just as she was about to put the milk on to simmer, the door was knocked on.

Seeing that it was a little after nine, she was tempted to ignore it, but then thought better of it.

She walked toward the door, and checked through the peephole to find Steven on the other side.

Opening the door, she stared at him. "Hey."

"Hey, is it okay if I come in?"

"Lacey and Whizz aren't home."

"I know. I just heard, and I figured you'd want the company."

"In case the one-legged girl couldn't handle looking after her sister."

"You're more than capable of babysitting."

"I know, I know. I'm sorry. I'm just stressing at the moment."

"Do you have exams?"

"No. Well, in college you always have exams. They like to spring them on you when you least expect it. I'm good. I'm just a little tired. I've not been sleeping well just lately."

"You haven't?"

"A few pains. The cold never helps, and it's getting colder. I'll be fine in no time. Do you want some hot chocolate? You look like you need some."

"Yeah."

On the way into the kitchen, she had to grab the counter as pain rushed through her. The doctor said it was normal, especially toward the end of the night. She should probably remove her prosthetic, and rest. He always advised after a busy day to take it easy.

"Would you like me to finish the hot chocolate?" Steven asked, urging her to take a seat.

"Do you remember how Angel does it?"

"Sally, I've been doing hot chocolate with Angel for years. I was the first, original prospect that took care of Angel, okay."

"Wow, all that long ago. You must be old."

"I am, believe me. Way too old to be feeling the way I'm feeling."

"How are you feeling?" she asked.

Steven turned toward her. She felt his gaze deep down to her soul, stripping apart the layers of protection she'd been working tirelessly to put in place.

"You know how."

"Steven?"

"Look, I know there is a pretty big age gap."

"The age gap doesn't bother me, okay?" she said. There, she'd said it. Age didn't count to her. To Sally, it was about feelings. "I remember hearing you freak out a little at the thought that I may have a crush on you."

"You were fifteen, Sally. In case you didn't

notice, I'm ten plus years your senior. I could go to prison for fucking grooming or some shit."

She frowned. "You didn't even notice me, Steven. You were nice, and a friend. Might I also remind you that since I've been with The Skulls, I've not had any sexual experience at all? I'm twenty-one. You're not a criminal, and don't even for a second think you are."

"I hate it."

"What?"

"I want to go and find all the men that touched you, that hurt you."

Sally sighed. "It's all in the past. If you're looking for a woman who hasn't been touched before, then you're looking at the wrong girl. Shit happened to me when I was younger, and I was nervous around Whizz when I saw him. Men in general scared me. The Skulls, you've all given me reason to see that it wasn't my fault. I don't want to talk about this. I've done the whole counseling thing, and it doesn't work. Constantly moving forward, never looking back. That's what works, and I lied to you."

"When?"

"I had the biggest crush on you, and I didn't understand it. You were nice, and you didn't treat me like a kid, or show pity toward me. You were just you, and I liked that. Besides, you know you're a hot guy as well. I had a crush on you."

"Sally, are you okay?" Daisy asked, calling downstairs.

"Two seconds."

She left Steven to think about what she said, walking toward the stairs. Her sister held onto her teddy bear, looking concerned.

"You were yelling."

"Oh, sweetie." Slowly, she climbed the stairs.

"Steven's being a silly boy again."

"Mommy says he's a weirdo."

"Mommy is always right, and so is Daddy. Come on. I can't pick you up tonight, Daisy."

"Your knee hurts?"

"It really does." Taking Daisy's hand, Sally helped her back into bed. Pressing a kiss to her brow, she smiled down at her little sister.

Neither of them were related, not by blood, but to Sally that didn't matter.

"You need to get some sleep, princess. You've got a long day ahead of you. Remember, we plotted mischief."

"And mayhem."

"Exactly."

"Sally," Daisy said.

"Yeah, would you wish for another sister?"

"What? No. Don't ever think that okay? You're my sister, and I love you so much."

"A boy at school. His name is Brandon, said that I was a horrible girl, and that no one would ever want to be my friend because I smell like dog poo."

Sally chuckled. "That's okay. Girls are so totally awesome. He smells like poo. Not us. Besides, if we do, we'd still smell awesome."

"I love you, Sally."

"Love you, too, pumpkin."

Leaving the bedroom, she got to the stairs, and sighed. Bum shuffling down them would do. Sitting on her ass, she started to move downstairs. Seconds passed, and Steven was there.

"What are you doing?"

"It's the best way to get downstairs, when I don't have any faith in my leg."

He walked up, holding her in his arms, and

carrying her back down to the stool in the kitchen. "Or sometimes you could just ask for help."

Steven pressed a kiss to her nose. "I have a confession to make," he said.

"You do."

"I have a crush on you as well."

Oh boy!

Chapter Eight

Later that night, Baker escorted Millie down to the restaurant. They had already gotten the call from Alex and Sunshine that they had arrived and would be meeting them for dinner.

Butch and Cheryl would be arriving with them. Ned was once again on babysitting duty.

Ned Walker, Eva's father and Tiny's father-in-law, really was a force to be reckoned with. Everyone feared him, and most adored him.

Baker was heading toward the bar in the restaurant when he caught sight of his four friends.

Sunshine smiled at Millie, and the two shared a quick hello.

Helping her into her seat, Baker nodded at Butch and Alex.

"How's the penthouse?" Alex asked.

"It's perfect, Alex, thank you so much," Millie said.

"Only the best for friends. I have to say I expected some other news to come home by now," Alex said.

"News?"

"Yes. You, Baker, Vegas, a potential wedding."

Baker chuckled.

"Why is everyone trying to marry us off?"

"They want us to be exactly like them, sweetie," Baker said, kissing her shoulder.

"What's wrong with us wanting to see you both happy? You've both got a right to it," Sunshine said. "I've never seen you like this, Baker. It's nice. The smile works for you."

Baker kissed Millie's head. "We're not getting

married. At least not this weekend."

She turned toward him. "Is that some kind of proposal?"

"Nope. It's a promise that it's still on the cards to do."

"Wow, is it?"

"What else do you think will happen?" He stroked her cheek. "We're good together, you know that."

He watched as her eyes dilated, giving away her aroused state.

"I'm starting to think The Skulls men are a little too confident," she said.

"That you've got right," Alex said, raising his glass. "To The Skulls."

They all raised their glasses, sharing a toast.

"So, is there anything back home I should know about?" Baker asked.

"Whizz has been happy to inform me that Lash is perfectly well, and that he has a scheduled vasectomy."

Baker spit his drink into his glass. "What?"

"Yeah, it seems the good Prez is so concerned with Angel and her giving birth that he's taking the decision out of her hands."

"No, it's not just that. Whizz is being a girl, gossiping about everything."

"I think I take offense to that. What about you girls?" Cheryl asked.

"I have to agree. In all of the years I've known The Skulls, the men do like to gossip," Millie said.

Baker looked at his woman.

"What? You can't give me that look. That time you were luring me to have dinner with Hardy and Rose. You were always talking about their relationship, and how Hardy wanted to try and mend the heartache between them."

"I wasn't gossiping."

"You were talking about the relationship of someone else, gossiping. You see, women have more important things to discuss," Millie said.

"Exactly. Like which brand of food mixer is the best," Sunshine said.

"Or what brand of marinara sauce tastes the best," Cheryl said.

"Or what should I get my husband for his birthday. He has everything he wants." This from Millie. "We don't gossip, and if we did, I doubt it would go in our partner's favor."

"Hell no, Butch leaves the toilet seat up," Cheryl said.

"Alex drinks out of the milk carton. I hate it. Why can't he get a glass?"

"Baker constantly complains about the cake he eats at the coffee shop."

"It was too dry," Baker said. He knew his cakes, and when one was overbaked. He'd paid four dollars for a slice of cake that was overbaked, and the icing hadn't been properly mixed. He was pissed.

"I was thirsty, and the glasses are the opposite side of the kitchen," Alex said.

"I've got no excuse. I leave the toilet seat up," Butch said.

Baker glared at him.

"What?" Butch held his hands up in surrender. "I'm going to own up to the shit I do. I'm a good guy like that."

"You're a kiss ass. That's what you are."

"Thank you." Butch kissed Cheryl's cheek. "See, I'm a kiss ass. You can't be mad at me for all the time."

"I can be mad at you if I want to."

Millie chuckled. "You're cute. You're a cute couple."

"Thank you."

"We got way off track with that conversation," Alex said. "I will report to the others to remove all decorations, streamers, and other paraphernalia. You're not getting married."

"Not yet," Baker said. "I'm going to hope that one day she'll change her mind."

Millie leaned in close, resting her head on his shoulder.

"We're taking it slow. I hope."

"When are you two heading back home?" Alex asked.

"Friday." Baker answered easily.

"Good, Angel wanted me to extend an invitation to the two of you. Sunday lunch, The Skulls' place. She's doing all the cooking." He turned to Butch and Cheryl. "You two can come, too."

"Thank you for the invite, but right now, I'd really rather not travel," Cheryl said, touching her stomach.

"Are congratulations in order?" Alex asked.

"Yes, we're hoping so."

"Then congratulations. I'll let everyone at the club know of the good news."

"We're hoping it's good news this time."

"This time?" Sunshine asked.

"We've had a few problems," Butch said.

Baker saw the pain between the two, and he knew part of what they were going through.

"To the future," he said.

He really hoped Butch and Cheryl found happiness, and that their baby came into the world, sprightly and bouncing.

The rest of the meal went by without any hitches. It was the first time that Baker could recall seeing Cheryl and Alex be in the same room without exchanging cross words. He was impressed.

Instead of staying for coffee, he saw Cheryl really wanted some alone time with Sunshine and Alex, so Baker said his goodbyes.

With a hand on Millie's back, he took her back to their penthouse suite.

"Is everything okay, do you think?" Millie asked.

"I'm hoping so. I don't like the thought of any of my friends being in pain." He followed her into the bathroom, loving the fact she was getting undressed even with him in the same room. "Can I say, I love your ass?"

"My ass now? I thought you liked my breasts."

"Tits, ass, I don't care, I love all of it."

Wrapping his arms around her, he breathed in her scent.

After so much pain in his past, he never thought he'd find love again, and yet he had, with a gorgeous, shy, toy shop owner.

****

"What's wrong?" Alex asked, getting straight to business. They didn't have time to talk before coming to the restaurant, and he wasn't interested in waiting around, or beating around the bush.

Cheryl had contacted him a few days ago asking if they could have a talk. He didn't know what that meant, but instantly his fears went toward his son.

"There's something I want to talk to you about," Cheryl said.

"You can say no," Butch said.

"Why don't you tell me what it is, and then I can decide what to do."

"Sweetie, there's no need to panic," Sunshine

said.

His wife gave his hand a squeeze, offering him comfort. "You're right. I'm sorry. I've just been out of my mind with worry."

"Worry, oh, I'm so sorry. Everything is fine. I mean, Michael, he's a handful right now. A real handful, and Ned is doing all he can."

"We're worried about him falling into the wrong crowd, while he's here," Butch said.

"He's becoming very disrespectful. Not just to teachers, but also to Butch."

Butch smiled, looking at Alex. "You can't tell me what to do, you're not my dad. My dad would kick your ass."

"Wow. That doesn't sound like the boy I know."

Cheryl had tears in her eyes. Alex was immune to her feelings. His love was for Sunshine. Sleeping with Cheryl had been a mistake, and having Michael, was also a mistake, but it was a mistake that he loved. He'd missed so much of Michael's early years.

"We're not trying to get rid of him. Just, I want to protect him, Alex. You're his father, and I know you'll do right by him."

Alex frowned. "What exactly are you asking?"

"I was wondering if you'd like for Michael to come and live with the two of you, for a little while. I think one of the reasons he's acting up is because we moved away from you. He misses you, Alex. You're his father, and I'd rather him be in Fort Wills with the other Skulls, than here."

"There are a couple of gangs here."

"We'd be happy to have him, and of course, we'll be open to you guys visiting whenever you wanted," Sunshine said.

Words had failed him.

"I'd like to talk to Michael about it."

"Yes, that's fine. I expected as much. It would have to be tomorrow morning now. I hope that is okay."

"Yes, it is."

Later that evening, Alex stared at his wife where she lay on the bed. She wasn't sleeping. Her dark skin beckoned for him to go to her, but he held back. Finally, she opened her eyes, staring at him.

"You're frowning again. You keep doing that, and you'll get wrinkles."

"I already have wrinkles."

"Not lots of them." She moved to her knees, and reached out, stroking his forehead. "Why are you frowning?"

"Nothing, just thinking about Michael. If he wants to come home with us, are you okay with that?"

"Alex, he's your son."

"With another woman. Some women would have a problem with that."

"You've got me. I'm totally angry."

"I'm being serious."

"I'm fine with it. He's still just a child, Alex. He's your son, and I love you. He needs you."

"I won't have him disrespecting you."

"I'm an awesome person. Just watch, I'll win over your son. I'll be the cool stepmom."

Wrapping his arms around her, he pulled her to her feet. "Show me how awesome you think I am."

"Certainly, sir." She batted her eyes, and he groaned as she pressed her soft body against him.

****

The following morning, Alex took Michael out for pancakes. He stopped at an old fifties style dinner. It had been a couple of months since he'd last seen his son, and even in that time, he'd grown up so much.

"So, how are you doing?" he asked.

"Okay, I guess. Are you going home today?"

"Well, that's up to you really."

"Me?"

Alex took a sip of his coffee.

"I want to know what you think of something."

Michael stared across at him, looking completely bored out of his mind. "I'm waiting."

Oh, this kid had attitude. That was fine. Alex wasn't worried about a little trouble.

"How would you feel to coming back to Fort Wills with me and Sunshine? You live with me, go to school with the other Skulls kids."

Michael snorted. "Yeah, as if Mom would ever go for something like that, or Butch."

"Actually, it was your mother's idea."

His son sat stunned. "It was?"

"Yes. It would seem that you've become quite a handful while here, and you're more susceptible to peer pressure. She wants you to be around the right kind of people." Alex folded his arms, staring at his son.

"I would love to. I'll do anything."

"You'd do anything to come and live with me?"

"Yes. I want to go back to Fort Wills. I don't want to live here anymore. I hate it here."

Alex accepted the pile of pancakes from the waitress, waiting for her to leave. "Why the sudden hatred of Vegas, and Butch?"

Michael took a bite of his food, and ate with his mouth open.

"Close your mouth when you're chewing. You may think you look like a punk, but it's gross, and makes you look stupid." He wouldn't allow his son to walk all over him. Unlike Butch, he *was* Michael's father.

"Are you just going to be a drag? Telling me

what to do, how I should look?"

Alex took a bite of buttery pancake and stared at his son. He didn't stop staring, waiting until Michael caved, averting his gaze. "You can talk the talk, but you can't walk the walk."

"Ned has been training me."

"A few weeks under Ned's training, and you think you're ready to take on me." Alex tilted his head. "You really do have a piss poor attitude, don't you?"

"Look—"

"If you think for one second you're going to get away with shit because I'm your dad and I've been absent, think again. You will show me and Sunshine respect. If you think to be a little shit to your sister, I will make your life a misery."

"Yeah, by doing what?"

"I can send you to military school, or better yet, unleash The Skulls on you. I'm not talking the older generation either. The new generation, they're lethal, and they'll chew you up, and spit you back out."

Michael stared.

"Your attitude sucks. It ends now, or your ass will be dropped at the nearest school."

"Mom won't let that happen."

"She won't have a choice. She's pregnant, and I'd say you being the way you are, you'll hurt her."

Michael went pale. "No, I wouldn't."

"You think stress is good for a woman? It can be the cause of so much crap. Women have died while carrying a baby."

Alex allowed his warning to sink in. Michael pushed his pancakes around. "I won't be disrespectful. I'll behave, and I'll be good."

"Excellent. Now tell me what the hell went wrong with Butch."

"He's the reason we're here. You left Vegas, and live in Fort Wills. I don't want to live here. I hate it here."

"Stop being a little brat, and grow up. Life is hard, Michael. It's not going to be easy. I wish there was something I could do, but there isn't. Butch is making the most of the situation. The least you can do, is help them. They're hurting. Butch is your stepparent. He doesn't have to give a shit, but he does. So does Sunshine. You have four parents, Michael. Two extra than most. For some, you have four extra than most. Stop taking everything for fucking granted. Now eat your damn pancakes."

****

The week flew by, and all too soon Millie was back in her apartment, wishing for the week to happen again.

"I loved our time together," she said.

"Good, I loved being with you. It was nice to get away," Baker said.

"It's going to be a long and busy day tomorrow." She'd dumped her washing beside the machine. Besides opening up the shop, and giving it a bit of airing, she had a week's worth of washing to do.

"How about we prolong today, and go out to the club? Go and see everyone. It's Friday, and there'll be a little get-together. There always is."

"You'd like to take me to one of your parties?"

"I think it's about time I do."

Millie bit her lip.

"What is it?" he asked.

"Could you pick me out something to wear? I don't know what to put on."

"Easy. Just go with jeans, a sweater, and a jacket. It's too damn cold to have anything else on."

An hour later, they were heading out to the club, ready to have some food. She was starving, and nervous about getting together with The Skulls. The last time it had been a family get-together, there had been a drive by shooting. Happy, one of the club prospects who was a previous nomad, had gotten killed. There had also been a lot of people injured.

They drove in the car, and she was sure Baker was missing his bike. For a week he'd not taken it for a ride.

Entering the parking lot, she saw there was a fire glowing at the back, past the children's playground that had been put in. There were a lot of kids at The Skulls, and with it came a lot of babysitting. The guys had all banded together to put one in so it made looking after children easier. Of course, come the winter when it was all slippery with ice, it wasn't such a good idea.

Climbing out of the car, Baker came toward her, taking her hand. The nerves were eating away at her. A couple of scantily clad women called toward Baker. He ignored them, going toward the back. She spotted Nash and Sophia first. They were cuddled up on the ground, drinking from a steaming thermos. Whizz and Lacey were next. Prue and Zero were snuggled, along with Tate and Murphy. Killer and Kelsey were wrapped around each other, dancing, as were Emily and Blaine.

"Who is on kiddy duty tonight?" Baker asked.

"Eva and Tiny," Angel said, carrying out a large tray. Several bowls were loaded with what looked like chili.

Baker let her go, grabbing two bowls. "I promised I'd feed you."

"Thank you." She took one of the bowls, and took a bite, moaning as the food exploded flavor on her tongue.

"I've been practicing my recipe for it. I want it to be perfect. I even have a child friendly chili," Angel said.

"She really does. Simon loves it," Tate said. "I've never seen him eat a bowl of the stuff so fast."

"It's Anthony's favorite."

"You do love kids, don't you, Angel?" Whizz said.

"Yes, of course I do." She smiled at Lash.

Millie recalled what Alex had said, and wondered if Angel knew the truth of what Lash was planning. From the look in her eye, Millie doubted it.

"Would you like more kids?" Lacey asked.

"Let's not talk about that right now," Lash said. "How was your trip? Alex told us you had no intention of actually getting married."

"It was a shame. I had the decorations in place," Angel said, moving toward them. She pulled Millie into a hug. "I'm teasing you. I didn't think you'd get married like that."

"No, Millie deserves a white wedding, right?" Whizz asked.

She turned to the heavily scarred man. "Erm, not really. I don't see the need to go to that expense."

"You little shit, you snooped, didn't you?" Baker asked.

"I may have had a little look." Whizz held up his hand with his thumb and finger close together.

Lash snorted. "A little? He has a full file."

"You fucker." Baker turned to her. "I didn't ask for it, I swear."

Millie frowned. "I don't have a clue what is going on. Snooping, files, I don't get it."

"I looked into your life, sweetie," Whizz said.

Lacey slapped him round the back of the head. "You didn't tell me you snooped on Millie?"

"It wasn't ever going to mean anything," he said.

"You looked at my life?" she asked. Millie wasn't stupid. The girls talked while they were ordering the toys, and the occasional gift for their husbands. She knew Whizz was a computer genius, and expert hacker. He helped to stop Andrew, and he helped that girl who now lived with Chaos Bleeds, Lola Sparks.

Everyone turned to Whizz. "Yeah."

"That wasn't exactly nice."

She looked at Baker.

"It wasn't me."

"It's fine. He probably found out how lame my life actually is."

"It really is. No porn or sex shop history at all." That earned Whizz another slap from Lacey.

Millie chucked. "My family has a lot of drama though, right?"

"Drama? They could make a soap opera about the shit that your family gets up to."

"You're not mad?" Baker asked.

"Nope. I've got nothing to hide. I told you the truth."

"So he knows about your previous ex-fiancé?" Whizz asked.

"I met him," Baker said. "Yes, in Vegas."

"It had to be one of the most awkward moments of my life," Millie said. "We also saw Butch and Cheryl."

"She's pregnant," Baker said.

"Michael is settling in. He didn't get off to a good start though," Angel said, wincing.

"He didn't?"

"Nope," Lash said.

"They still won't tell us what he did wrong," Tate said. "I tried getting it out of Simon, but his lips are sealed."

"Neither is Anthony talking," Angel said.

"Or Daisy," Lacey said.

"Neither is Darcy," Emily said.

"What happened?" Baker asked, chuckling.

"We don't know, apart from the fact that Tabitha kicked Michael in the nuts, then Darcy slapped him, and Simon punched him. Anthony shoved him, and when Michael was on the ground, they all proceeded to jump on him."

"Michael was saying horrible things. Called Tabitha ugly, Daisy fat, Simon small, and Miles lame. He then told them all that he was number one because he was the oldest, at which point, Darcy wasn't having him outrank her, and so, they pummeled him," Sally said, using her crutches to walk toward them. Steven was behind her, staring intently.

"How the fuck did you find that out?" Nash asked.

"Easy, I'm one of them, or at least that is what they say." Sally smiled. "They're Skulls through and through. Daisy told me that what Anthony said as a warning to Michael. They may be young, and they may not be perfect, but they're Skulls, they're family, and if you take on one, you take on them all, and then you're in big trouble."

"Wow," Lash said, puffing out his chest. "I'm a proud father."

"Michael is in for a rough ride," Whizz said. "He called Daisy fat?"

"Yeah, and Anthony didn't like that. Apparently Daisy was crying to Tabitha, and Anthony heard it. He then went back to Michael, sat on him, and forced him to eat dirt." Sally looked at Lacey and Whizz. "Don't worry, I spoke to Daisy. I told her she was fine, and she didn't need to worry. Boys suck, and she should know she's awesome."

Lacey looked relieved. "No one would say anything to us."

"They have a Skulls kids' vow. The grownups should never know. Don't tell them I told you." Sally winced. "Holy crap, I'm a grownup now. When did that happen?"

"Welcome to the club," Baker said.

The look of shock made Millie laugh. She loved the club. They were all amazing, loving, and a family. A real family as well. Her own family were nothing like The Skulls. There was no love. Everyone had to take care of themselves, and she hated it. Bethany, her sister, was never there for her, nor were her parents.

"Millie, you're big enough to fight your own fight!"

"Millie, for God's sakes. Do it yourself."

She'd never had a parent come to school, and none of them wanted to know of her success. Her grades were mocked.

"Are you okay, baby?" Baker asked.

"Yeah, I am." She snuggled in close to him, basking in the feeling that only he inspired.

Chapter Nine

Three months later

Baker stared at the apartment the realtor was showing him. It was on the sixth floor, and the view across the horizon was just beautiful. He needed to find his own place. Well, it wasn't *needed*, but it was something he wanted. When it came between him and Millie, he either spent time with her at her place, or she stayed at the clubhouse.

It was time for him to have his own place. Ever since he'd been prospecting with The Skulls, he'd been living at the clubhouse, and wasn't interested in finding another place to call his own.

When Katie died, he'd sold his business and the house. He'd gotten rid of everything, including furniture.

"This is the only apartment left," the realtor said.

He couldn't remember the woman's name, and he wasn't interested in remembering. Listening to the crap that came with selling any kind of property, he looked around. "There's no furniture?"

"No. It's entirely up to you, and the price does reflect that there is no furniture."

"If I accept, how soon until I can move in?"

"It depends on your loan."

"I'm a cash buyer," he said. He had plenty of money saved up. This place was well within his means, and he'd still have plenty left over. There was no reason for him to spend money in the past few years. What was the point? There was nothing to spend it on.

"Oh, well in that case, by the end of the month."

"Just in time for Halloween," he said.

"Yes, are you thinking of having a party?"

He saw the change in the woman immediately.

Staring at her, Baker frowned. Why? Was it because he was paying by cash? Did he suddenly look more attractive to her?

"I'll be spending it with my woman. I'll take it."

The realtor looked a little disappointed, but he didn't care. Millie was the only one for him, and that was the way it was going to stay.

The club, he saw it meant so much to her. The Skulls had always been a family. Even when they had more trouble than any of them could deal with, they stuck together and got through it. There was no other way to be.

Once he finished with the paperwork, he headed out toward his bike in time to see Gash arriving. His club brother lived in the same building, along with Charlotte.

"You checked the apartment already?" Gash asked.

"Yeah."

"Charlotte called me like ten minutes ago."

"It didn't take long for me to decide what I wanted."

"Does Millie know you're wanting to take that next step?" Gash asked, arms folded.

Baker shrugged. "It doesn't really matter. This place is for me. I've been putting it off for so long. I feel that it's time to have a space of my own, you know?"

"Yeah, I do. Living at the clubhouse has its perks, but I like coming home. It helps when you've got a woman to come home to."

He and Millie had been together for over three months now, and during that time, Baker had never been happier. For him, it was the strangest feeling in the world. Millie called to him in ways that Katie had not. There was no way he was ever going to compare the two. Millie was a sweetheart, and even though Katie had been, too, she's been more fired up, more passionate about being successful, which he'd loved about her then. Baker remembered how many times Katie would sit him down talking about how best to improve the bakery, what to do to get maximum price.

There were times she'd kind of sucked the fun out of baking, but that had been fine. He was young, determined to make his way in the world. They were both equals in that.

With Millie, she was different, or maybe he was different now. She didn't beg him to start his own job, nor did she try to convince him to start baking again. When he was with Katie, he'd been in a different place emotionally. Now, he was older, wiser, and he wanted different things out of life. The two people he'd been, Jaxson and now Baker, were not the same. He was the same, but what he wanted out of life was not. With Millie, he talked about what he did for The Skulls, going between their businesses, and helping to keep employees up to date with changes. Everyone at the club pitched in.

"You okay?" Gash asked.

"Yeah, yeah, I'm fine. I'm just having one of this moments, thinking about Katie."

"Katie? Who the fuck is Katie? You already straying from Millie?"

"No. Katie is my dead wife."

Gash stared at him. "Oh, I didn't even know her name. Sorry."

"Don't worry about it. I've not mentioned it before." Baker took a deep breath.

"What were you thinking?"

"Just how different she is from Millie. How different I am now, compared to then. I didn't even think I'd changed that much but I have."

"Why dwell on that shit? None of us are ever the

same people, Baker. You loved her, right?"

"Yeah, I did."

"Then don't think about anything else. Don't compare. Besides, you don't want to ruin your chances with Millie. She's a good woman, but from what I've seen of her, she's been hurt before." Gash slapped him on the back. "Are you sure you're ready?"

"What do you mean?"

"I know everyone wants you and Millie to get together, but if you're not ready, then don't take that next step. I like Millie, and I'd hate to see her hurt, but you're also my club brother, Baker. Don't do anything that you're going to regret."

"You think she's the rebound?"

"I don't know, you tell me?"

"Gash, Millie is the furthest thing from the rebound."

"I don't want to see you hurt, Baker. Your wife, she meant a lot to you."

"She really did, but I also know that a dead wife won't keep me warm at night. I want Millie. She…" He tried to find the right word to describe Millie. The way she made him feel was whole, complete. "She's everything, Gash. Everything, and just thinking about her makes me smile."

"You're ready?"

"More ready than I'll ever be. I love her." He smiled. "I'm in love with her."

Gash chuckled. "It's really something when you realize the truth, isn't it?"

"Holy shit, I love her, and I've wasted so fucking much time." He shook his head. "I've got to go and see her."

"Go ahead."

****

Gash watched him go, happy to see the true happiness within his friend. Heading up to his apartment, he opened the door, and Charlotte threw herself at him.

"Hello, big boy," she said.

"Well, hello. Did someone miss me?"

"Only a little but there's something I wanted to tell you," she said.

"And what's that?"

Charlotte took his hand and led him into the bathroom. He didn't know what was wrong or what was happening.

"I've not had my period in two months, and I took a test this morning while you were out." She handed him a white stick. "It's positive, Gash. We're going to have a baby."

Happiness swamped him, totally consumed him until he couldn't be sure if it was a dream or not.

"You're pregnant?"

"I'm pregnant. We're going to have a baby."

Gash gasped, then screamed before picking her up, and spinning her around. "We're going to be parents. We're going to have a baby."

Placing her on her feet, he cupped her face, tilting her head back, and kissing her. "I love you, Charlotte. I love you so fucking much."

"We're going to have a family, finally after all this time." She kissed him back with a passion that took his breath away. "I never thought we'd get another chance."

"I knew we would. Andrew took away our happiness, but I wouldn't allow him to ruin our future." He'd die for Charlotte, and for their unborn baby. Gash lowered himself to the floor and kissed her stomach. "You hear that, sweetie? You're going to be so spoilt."

"What do you want? Boy or girl?"

"I really don't care. I just want him or her to be healthy. I'll have a healthy baby. Everything else doesn't matter."

"We've got to tell the others," Charlotte said.

"Halloween is not far. How about we break it to them for the party?" This year Lacey had gotten her way, and the whole of The Skulls were having a Halloween party, complete with costumes, and a freaky inspired menu, including a monster meatloaf head. Gash didn't have a clue what that meant, but it all sounded like fun, and right now in his life, he wanted fun. More fun than anything else.

****

Millie was serving a customer as Baker walked in the shop. She saw the happiness in his eyes, and the excitement he was trying to contain.

"Now that guy looks hot," the woman said.

She chuckled. "That man is mine." Millie had never been one to actually make a claim on a man. When it came to Baker, he wasn't just any man. He was *the man*.

"You lucky woman."

Millie thought so, and waited for her customer to leave before turning to Baker. "You look perky this morning."

"I am. I've just bought something, and I'm pretty excited about it."

"What did you buy?"

"I bought an apartment."

"An actual apartment?" Millie asked. "I thought you lived at the clubhouse."

"I do, and I can still live there, but it's not what I want for the rest of my life. I was hoping you'd be willing to move in with me?"

The large stack of cards she'd been carrying

tumbled around her as she spun around. "Move in with you?"

"Yes. It's the next step, and I really want a place to call our own."

"You can move into my place?"

"Millie, you hate it up there. You've not put much in the way of personal touches, and I know you like getting up and going to work, but think about it. Come and stay with me for a couple of weeks. What do you say?" Baker took her hands, pulling her against him.

"You don't think we're moving too fast?" she asked.

Was it too much to hope they could be moving forward? Not only was it the past three months they'd been dating, and doing some pretty damn heavy petting, but it had been over three years of waiting for Baker. Nearly five years of waiting for him, and she was done waiting.

She was a twenty-nine year old virgin, scared to take that next step.

Life was passing her by, and being around The Skulls, and witnessing them in the past three months up close and personal, she knew without a doubt, she wanted that connection with someone.

"I don't think we're moving too fast. If I'm being truthful, I don't think we're moving fast enough, Millie. Time is flying by, and I don't want to wake up regretting another moment."

"Do you regret already?"

"Yes. I regret holding onto the memory of Katie. I regret leaving this between us for so long. I could understand you though. I know you now more than ever before. No one has ever wanted you for you, and because of that, you've never felt what it is like to be wanted, to be needed, and to be loved. I can give you all of those things, but it requires something from you."

He cupped her face, tilting her head back, and Millie could do no more than stare into his eyes.

"What?"

"To take a leap of faith with me. To ride this wave no matter what. I know there will be pain along the way, and a few disappointments. Life always is, but I can promise you I won't want another woman, I won't be comparing you to anyone else, and it'll just be you and me. Are you ready for that?"

She licked her suddenly dry lips.

"Tonight, Baker, I want you to make love to me. I want you to be my first."

Millie saw she had surprised him. "What?"

"I'm ready. I'm more than ready. I have to be the oldest virgin living, and I don't want that title anymore. I want to get rid of it. I want my first time to be with you."

Baker slammed his lips down on hers, sliding his tongue across before she opened up, moaning as he thrust inside.

She moaned, meeting his tongue with hers, dancing together to their beat.

"Tonight?" he asked.

"Tonight. You and me. No complications."

"I don't own the apartment yet."

"No, here. I'll make us dinner, and if you'd like, you can stay the night."

"Are you on the pill?" he asked.

"No. I'm not. I've always had a reaction to the pill. It doesn't like me."

"I'll take care of it." He pressed his lips to hers again. At the same time, the door opened and closed. "Tonight."

She watched him leave. Her heart was pounding, and she did her best to ignore the nerves that was currently rushing through her entire body. Holy shit, what had she done?

It's okay.

You want this.

Your first time is going to be with Baker.

Your only times will be with him.

Her lips were sore, and she made her way over to the older woman who came into the store.

After twenty minutes of helping her pick out the best gift for a grandson, Millie rushed to close the shop. Once that was done, she grabbed her cell phone, and dialed Lacey's number.

"Pick up. Pick up. Pick up."

"Hello, sweetie, what can I do for you today?"

"I've just asked Baker to make love to me tonight, and I'm freaking out. I mean seriously freaking out. What do I do?" Millie asked. "I want to look … good. Nice down there, and all over."

"Wait? You and Baker haven't done it yet?"

"No."

"Why not?"

Even though they were not in the same room, Millie's cheeks heated at Lacey's question. "Erm, I'm sort of a virgin, and it's no big deal. I mean, the first time is no big deal."

"You're a virgin!" Lacey yelled the words so that Millie had no choice but to hold the cell phone away from her ear.

"Yeah, just tell everyone."

"Right, you need to go upstairs, shower, and wash, and stay in a towel. I'll be there with a few reinforcements."

"Reinforcements? I don't like that. What the hell?"

"Just, don't worry about it. I'll handle

everything."

"Lacey?"

"Yep."

"Try and keep the whole virgin thing to yourself."

"Sure, sure."

Millie hung up the phone, knowing without a doubt that everyone close to her would know she was a virgin, or at least her days of being a virgin were in fact numbered. Thirty minutes later, there was a knock on her door, and she made her way down, dressed in only a robe. Lacey, Kelsey, and Angel were the only three there.

"This is it?"

"I'll need some help, and besides, there may be a couple more people turning up. This is a big deal, a huge event for you, and you need your besties to help me through it," Lacey said.

"Besties?" Millie followed them upstairs.

"Best friends," Angel said. "We're your support group."

"I've never had a support group." She'd not really had much of anything.

"Well, now you have. The Skulls, we stick together. The club, the women, and even the kids," Kelsey said. "We're all a little shocked that you're a virgin."

"All?" Millie asked.

"Yeah, I had to call Angel, so Lash picked up. I told him it was an emergency, and it sort of slipped."

"'Virgin end mission' is not exactly letting it slip," Angel said.

"What's the big deal? It's not like I told anyone outside of the club."

"Yeah, only Baker's going to be getting ribbed for it. You did it on purpose," Kelsey said. "You're always stirring trouble."

"Wait, that would be Tate and Prue. I'm innocent. Besides, the club is your family, sweetie. It's time you realized it. You're not alone. You'll never be alone, and we'll all be here to make sure you're happy."

Tears filled Millie's eyes. "Thank you. I don't really know what to say."

"Well, good for you, I'm awesome, and I have no problem asking Baker what his personal preferences are."

"Preferences?" Millie asked, feeling entirely out of her depth, especially with all of the questions Lacey was asking.

"Yeah, if he likes you bare, or with a little hair." Lacey pointed between her thighs.

"Wait a minute. Wait a minute. Nothing is happening to my girly parts. I just freaked out, and I want to look nice. I'm happy with my woman's bits, and that is not going to be changing. You can keep those hands, and razors, and scissors, and ouch, waxes to yourself."

Lacey sighed. "Fine, fine, he did say he was more than happy with the way you are. It's good to know what your man wants. Some men like you to be bare, some with a lot of hair, some with a little. It's a very picky environment."

Millie sat down, covering her face. "Why did I call you?"

Everyone started laughing.

"Lacey grows on you. Once you realize she doesn't have any kind of filter. It's funny to watch her get into all kind of problems," Kelsey said.

"I feel like I'm always calling you guys to come and help."

"It's what we want to do," Angel said. "I want to see you and Baker happy. You both deserve it."

"Baker's been miserable for far too long. Besides,

I kind of made a teeny, tiny bet."

"A bet?" Millie asked.

"Yep."

"Who with?" Angel asked.

"Whizz, my husband, who else. Anyway, I said that you're the one for Baker, and he thinks you're the one for Baker. The bet we have going on is if you'll be married before Christmas."

"What!"

"I think it'll be next year. He thinks you'll be married before Christmas. I'm wanting to help, so the lust stage, the sleeping together part helps me."

"How does it help you?" Angel asked.

"Simple. They're sleeping together, so the lust will drive them for the next couple of months. Then you'll have the manic of Christmas, to which you're invited. Angel's doing a big thing at the club. She does it nearly every single year. It's just a Skulls thing this year. Chaos Bleeds are coming for Thanksgiving. Then the new year will be here, and you have to marry."

"What do you win?" Millie asked.

Angel groaned. Kelsey giggled.

"Girls, nothing so dirty. We have virgin ears. A foot rub this time."

Millie looked at Kelsey and Angel seeing the relief on their faces. "She and Whizz have a tendency to bet certain sexual favors," Angel said.

"Once Lacey had to be his slave. Like a Dominant and submission thing," Kelsey said. "It was creepy."

"That was fun. We didn't use any toys or anything. I just had to do exactly as I was told, and ladies, there is a lot of fun in that as well."

Millie chuckled. These women, they were complete nut balls, but she loved them. Seeing the love and the friendship between them, even when they were bickering, Millie knew she would love to be part of that.

****

Tate stirred the stew, putting the lid back on the pan, and placing it in the oven. Wiping down the counter, she put items back into the sink and the ingredients back into place in the kitchen.

She did love to have a clean kitchen, where everything had its own place.

Murphy entered the kitchen through the back door. He'd already moved his boots and placed them on the back deck.

"That's all the leaves bagged up until the next wave hits."

"Can you believe we're at this place right now?" she said. "We're married, happily. Two children, one at school, the other having a nap? I'm standing at the stove, making stew."

"It does seem a bit surreal to me. I always knew we'd end up like this. It was only a matter of time of when." He moved behind her, wrapping his arms around her waist. Murphy kissed her neck and breathed in deeply. "To me, you've always been home."

"Speaking of home. It has been three months, Murphy." She turned in his arms. "Three months. Do you know what you want to do?"

He sighed. "Tate?"

"Murphy?"

"Why did you ask me this?" he asked.

"Because I've been the one making a lot of the decisions. It's time for you to start making them."

He started chuckling. "You really think you've been making decisions?"

"Yeah."

"Babe, I was the one that picked this house. I'm

the one that decided we were going to stay. I was the one who convinced you to get married. I was the one that knocked you up. I asked Angel to teach you how to cook. Everything we've done is because of me. I want to stay in Fort Wills. I want our kids to be near their grandparents. I want us to be near the people who have always had our back, no matter what." He stroked her cheek. "I've always picked here with you. If you want to move, then we can move. That decision is yours, and yours alone."

"Wait a moment, *I* picked this place."

"I kept putting the pamphlet where you could see it. It's perfect. We have a front and back yard, a nice decent sized kitchen, three bedrooms, a sitting room, dining room, two bathrooms. You tell me what could be more perfect?" he asked.

She opened her mouth, and closed it. "Wow, I didn't—"

"Do you want to leave all of this behind? I'll do everything for you, Tate."

"No, I don't. I really, I want to stay here." She wrapped her arms around his neck. "I thought it was all me."

"Not at all, baby. It was all me as well. This is our home, and it's our kids' home. I'll move, gladly for you."

"No. I don't even want to hear another word about moving. I love it here, and I love our family." Tate chuckled.

"What's Isabella doing?" Murphy asked.

"She's sleeping."

"Where?"

"In her room." She lifted up the little controller to show she was watching her.

"Baby, it has been too long since I've taken you anywhere but on the bed." Murphy picked her up and placed her on top of the counter. "And now I think it's time for me to have a little taste of you."

"Oh, Murphy, I don't mind that."

Chapter Ten

"There are several complaints at the gym about a Luke Pearlman," Baker said, handing over the file of complaints to Lash.

Lash rubbed at his temple. "He's the personal trainer, right?"

"Yeah, some of the women complain that he's too harsh, or nasty to them. He overworks them." Baker took a seat.

"It's a gym. Isn't that what they're paying the guy to do? To get them to work out or some shit."

Baker shrugged. "I don't know. I guess they'd rather him doing it nicely. Lilo, the woman working the front desk, she thinks it's because he's a hottie."

Lash rolled his eyes.

"Some cougar action going on."

"How old is this guy?"

"Thirty. Some of the women are late forties, early fifties. They don't seem to like his direct, hands on approach."

"It's not the hands on they want?"

"I don't know. Again, the workout I do is either running, or pressing weights. I don't go to the fucking gym and run on shit. Lame. What about you?"

"I've got some weights at home. I've got better ways of working out. It's just another list of shit to do."

"Going legit has its consequences."

"Was it like this at the bakery you owned?"

"Yep, tax sheets, income, expenses, product. You name it. Everything had to be accounted for, and of course there was a risk someone would complain about food tasting foul. It's a risk you take when you deal with food, and with all kinds of business. It's the headache."

Baker checked the time seeing it was past six. "Can I head out? I've got someplace to be."

"Yeah, deflowering Millie," Lash said.

Baker paused. "Come again?"

"Lacey can't keep her mouth shut, and it seems Millie wanted to look her best for you tonight."

"Do I even want to know how many people know?"

Lash shook his head. "We're a club and family for a reason. Go and get her, tiger."

"That is just wrong, totally wrong on so many levels."

Leaving the clubhouse, Baker didn't waste his time, and made his way toward Millie's apartment. He was nervous as fuck. Millie was a virgin, and even though she wasn't his first virgin, it was their first time. He wasn't a kid anymore either. When he'd been with Katie, they had both been eighteen. He knew more now, and he wanted to make this a night Millie would never forget. He was determined to do everything so that she'd remember it as the best night of her life, or at least the first in many to come.

Parking his bike outside of her shop, he saw that she had already closed the shop.

Taking a deep breath, he knocked on her door, and waited.

Seconds passed, and finally the door opened, showing him Millie. She was in a gorgeous blue dress that pushed her tits together, showing off an amazing cleavage. The dress only served to enhance her generous curves, highlighting her full hips and rounded stomach.

"Hello," she said.

She still wore those sexy glasses that he loved so damn much. They made her look so cute.

"Hey, baby," he said.

"Lacey was here."

"Lash told me."

She moved out of the way, and he entered the main hall.

"Did he tell you everything?" she asked. "They all know what is happening tonight?"

"Nothing is sacred at the club anymore. Everyone knows everyone else's business. I didn't say anything."

"I know. I kind of told Lacey, and she told everyone else."

He saw her cheeks were red. "No one will say anything. You don't have to worry about that. I mean the guys won't. I don't know what the girls will do."

She chuckled. "They've told me to call them in case anything goes wrong, and I freak out."

"I won't hurt you."

"I know." She touched his cheek. "Do you want to come on up? I made dinner."

He followed her upstairs. The scent of onions and garlic was heavy in the air. The small table she owned was set for romance. Two long candles were lit, and he saw wine glasses and plates.

"Will you take a seat?" she asked.

He caught her hand, pulling her against him. "If anything happens tonight that you don't want to, all you have to do is say, and I'll stop it."

She placed her hand on his chest. "You're the sweetest man ever." She gave him a quick kiss and entered her kitchen.

He removed his jacket, pleased that he'd actually changed before giving his report to Lash.

"Did you have a good day?" she asked.

"Yeah, I had to go over to the gym. One guy, Luke, has been getting some complaints."

"Luke Pearlman?" she asked.

"You know him?"

"Yeah, I've seen him around town. Also, some of the women that come into the shop like to gossip. He's a good man. I've heard wonderful things about him."

"Not from the complaints I've received." He gave her some of the comments that had appeared in the file.

"Wow, that doesn't sound like Luke at all. His job means everything to him."

"Either way, Lash has to look into it. The gym, it's only just turning a profit."

"I wonder why he'd be so mean." She came and took the plates. "Forgot I needed to serve dinner."

She was gone and back within seconds, taking a seat. "Spaghetti carbonara. I hope that is okay."

"It's perfect. It's one of my favorites. I drive Angel crazy with this request, especially when I'm ill."

"How come?"

"I'm ill, and cream, cheese, and somewhat raw egg, doesn't exactly help settle a stomach."

"Right, right."

He saw her hand was shaking a little, and he reached out, capturing her hand. "If you've changed your mind, tell me."

"No, I haven't changed my mind. I've just never gotten to this stage. When I went out with Brian, we'd see a movie, never have dinner. This is all new. Apart from Jack, he doesn't count."

"Brian was and is an asshole loser."

"Asshole loser, I like that one. Sorry if I keep repeating words. I suck sometimes. I told Sandy about Jack, and she didn't seem shocked by it at all."

"You don't suck, and Sandy can hold her own." Still holding her hand, he twirled the pasta, and took a bite. "Now that is perfection. It's official. You have to marry me."

"What! You want to marry me?" She looked shocked.

"You made the perfect pasta, I … adore you, and I think we're good together." Tonight was not the night to start talking about love. She wasn't ready, at least not yet. He was fine with that. He could wait.

"Everyone keeps talking about marriage."

"Everyone? You got a marriage proposal waiting for you?" he asked.

"No, Lacey. She was telling me she's got some kind of bet going on with Whizz about us getting married."

Baker rolled his eyes. "Those two are so meddling. What's the bet?"

She gave him the details, and by the end of it, they were both chuckling. "I really don't know what to make of that."

"A lot of The Skulls have gotten married at Christmas. I think it's some kind of omen."

"Omen, bad or good?"

"I'm hoping good. All of the couples are still together."

"Would you even like to get married again?" she asked.

"To the right woman, and if you asked me, then I'd say yes."

"You'd marry me?" she asked.

"Is that a proposal?"

"No. I'm not ready to get married. We've only been dating a few months, and we've not even had sex yet."

"Sex doesn't count in a marriage," he said.

"It doesn't? I thought it played a huge part."

Baker laughed. "It helps. Sex, it does help, but we're not going to spend twenty-four hours a day, seven days a week in a bed, screwing."

"We're not."

"You'll need to rest, and to recover. I believe there needs to be more between a couple. Talking, liking each other. When I'm with you, Millie, I don't want to be in silence. Those people that only use sex as a basis, I always wonder what more there is. Do they even talk between sex? Do they have sex, turn over, and ignore each other?"

"Texting each other on the phone? Or their friends?" she asked.

"Marriage is more than sex, way more. It's a partnership. It's a lifetime, and with it, there has to be a lot more than sex. Especially when I get really old and the old chap doesn't want to work." He winked at her. "I'm thinking over a hundred. Even though, Ned Walker is pushing it a bit, and he looks healthier than ever I've seen him."

"Ned's a darling."

"He's a ladies' man, and don't you forget it."

She chuckled, giving his hand a squeeze. "We've proven that there's more here than just sex."

"Even if I didn't get to be inside you tonight, Millie, this is enough."

"Do you even want that?" Millie asked. "Sex?"

"Baby, I want it. I want to be inside you so much I ache for it, but I also know that I can wait. You're worth waiting for."

He saw her eyes glistened, and she shook her head. "No, I'm not going to cry. I refuse to get emotional right now. This is a good night, and I'm happy. I really am happy. You make me this way, and I adore you, too, Baker. I really do."

They finished off their food, and Baker told her more about his day. He talked about everything but the night, and helped to calm her nerves. When the food was finished, he helped with the dishes, and finally, it was Millie who took his hand, and led him toward her bedroom.

"If you don't want to—"

She pressed her finger over his mouth.

"I want this, Baker. I do. Don't give me an out. Don't give me a reason to run and hide. I'm twenty-nine years old, and I want to be with you. For you to be my first."

She started at the buttons of his shirt, and slowly began to open them. His cock was already hard, but the moment she touched him, it got even thicker.

He removed the club, binding her hair on top of her head. The silky strands fell down around her, and he ran his fingers through the thick length.

****

I'm doing this.

I'm doing this.

Going to have sex with Baker.

Millie closed her eyes, releasing a little moan as he fisted her hair. He pulled her close, and she offered up her lips at the same time she pushed his shirt to the floor. Running her hand up his chest, she wrapped them around his neck, pressing her body against his.

One of his hands moved, and she heard something land on the bed.

Pulling away from him, she saw the wad of condoms. There had to be at least ten packets on the bed.

"Are you planning a long night?"

"I want to be prepared."

"You think it's going to be a good night?"

"I'm going to make it the best night of your life, Millie. Whenever you look at me, I want you to remember tonight, and get so damn wet and horny that you need to fuck me."

She gasped at the sudden burst of arousal through her body.

"You want that?"

"Hell yeah. When we're in a room full of people, and we can't do anything about it, and I get to watch your need for me building. I'll know you're so wet, and it'll feel so damn good." He kissed her neck, biting on her pulse. Every touch seemed to only enhance her need for him.

Her pussy was already slick, and she wanted him.

"What are you doing to me?" she asked.

"I'm getting you ready."

Baker took the zipper of her dress and started to lower it down her body. He'd seen her naked enough times, and she no longer felt the need to cover her body. He thought she was beautiful, and she wasn't going to hide, not from him.

The dress fell in a pool at her feet, and she stepped out of it, kicking it aside.

"I've not seen this," he said, putting a finger beneath the lace of her bra.

"It's new." A blue, lacy bra complete with matching panties. She gave a little twirl. "Do you like it?"

He cupped her tits, running his thumb across each nipple. "I love it. Do you have any idea how fucking sexy and beautiful you are?"

"No." When she was with Baker though, she felt like nothing on earth could touch her.

Baker let go of her breasts and moved behind her. He flicked the catch, and the bra fell forward, his hands capturing her breasts as if they were the cup of the bra. He pulled her back against him, rubbing his cock against her ass.

He was so hard, and she wanted him, and she wanted this. One of his hands moved from her breast down her stomach to cup her pussy. He moved beneath the lace, and his finger stroked through her slit.

Crying out, she leaned against him as he moved his finger up and down, over her clit.

"You're so wet for me."

"I want you, Baker," she said.

Reaching behind her, she worked on the belt that kept his pants up. She loved that he'd dressed up for her.

Suddenly, his hand was gone, and he spun her around. "Remove your glasses."

She took them off, placing them on the drawer beside her bed.

He beckoned her with the crook of his finger, tugging her in more ways than one.

Once she was in front of him, he grabbed her hips, and placed her on the bed so that she was sitting. He took a step back and began removing his belt. The slow dance, with his swaying hips tempted her.

"What are you thinking?" she asked.

"I hope you're having a good time." The pants were gone, and she saw the outline of his dick through the boxer briefs. Licking her suddenly dry lips, she had to wonder if he'd fit inside her, and knew it was stupid. Of course he would fit. This was the most natural thing in the world.

"I am."

The boxers went, and his cock sprang forward, showing off his impressive length. The tip was already coated in pre-cum.

He knelt in front of her, grabbing her thighs, and tilting her back so that she was flat on the bed. Baker tore her panties off, throwing them away. "I'll buy you new ones."

"I can't believe you just did that."

"Believe it, babe." He spread open her thighs, and then his mouth was on her. "This is all for you." He flicked her clit repeatedly before sucking the bud into his mouth. She moaned his name, unable to hold back as he tortured her clit. She loved it when his mouth was on her. To her, it felt much better than his fingers.

He opened the lips of her sex, and she couldn't help but watch as his tongue moved up and down, then circled around the clit. She was swollen and wet, her cream dripping down the crease of her ass as he continued to suck her pussy.

"Oh, God, I can feel it," she said, dropping to the bed. Arching up, she screamed his name as her orgasm took her by surprise startling her in its intensity.

"So fucking perfect, and beautiful." He growled the words against her flesh, flicking her clit one last time. "I'm going to spend a lot of time doing that to you. Your pussy tastes so good. I know I'm not going to want to stop at one taste. I'm, going to want more. So much more."

He took one of the condom packets, tearing into it. Millie could not do or say anything as she watched him, taking in every line, every tense, every muscle. Baker was one hot guy, and he was all hers.

Baker urged her up the bed so that she was lying against the pillows. He moved between her thighs, and then she felt him at her entrance.

"Unchartered terrain," she said.

"Are you making a joke?"

"You're going where no man has ever gone before, Baker."

"And no man will ever be again." In one thrust, he embedded his length inside her. The moment he pushed, he broke through her barrier, Millie gasped at the pain, and the feeling of being stretched. She'd known and expected the pain. He caught her hands, holding them tightly, as he took possession of her mouth. Through the pain he kissed her, making her forget and focus on the feel of his lips instead.

"There's only me, babe. No one else, just me," he said.

She held his hands, tightly. "Don't let me go."

"I won't. You're mine now. There's no turning back now."

Millie stared into his blue eyes, and couldn't think of anything else she wanted than to be with this man who owned her soul.

She thrust up against him, ready to take him.

"Are you sore?"

"I want you, Baker. Please, don't stop."

He placed her hands beside her head, keeping hold of her, and using her for leverage as he started to slowly thrust within her. It was short, shallow thrusts, going in and out. Millie didn't look away from him, marveling at the fact Baker was inside her, not only her body but also her heart.

"You're so tight, Millie. So tight, and so mine."

His thrusts changed, and he started to speed up. The pain inside her became pleasure, and with it, a soaring feeling of freedom. She met each of his strokes, not wanting the pleasure to end.

"Oh, fuck, baby, that feels so good," he said. "I'm never going to get tired of fucking you."

The headboard hit the wall, the sound of their lovemaking echoing around the room. This was her first time, with some pain, and she couldn't wait for the next time, or the one after that.

"I'm not going to last."

Baker thrust deep inside her, and she felt the

moment he found his release. His cock twitched, filling the condom as he came.

Afterward, he collapsed on top of her, his breath fanning her breast as he came down from his orgasm.

"I'm sorry," he said.

"What for?"

"I wanted you to come with me."

"I came before we had sex."

"It can happen during, providing the man you're with isn't too selfish."

"I don't think you're selfish, Baker."

"You don't."

"No, I thought that was perfect." She kissed the top of his head. "Can we do it again?"

****

Anthony and Chloe were in bed, and Angel grabbed the basket of washing, heading toward the laundry room. She paused when she saw Lash there, waiting. He was leaning against the dryer, glaring at something. The moment he saw her, the glare was gone.

"When did you get home?" she asked.

"Just. I let myself in the back. I'll mow the lawn tomorrow."

"It's supposed to rain tomorrow."

"Shit, you asked me to do the lawn didn't you?" he asked.

"A week ago. It's fine. You can't do it tomorrow. It'll look a mess. Last time I checked electricity and water don't mix," she said, smiling.

He nodded.

"What's wrong?"

"Nothing, babe."

"Don't you nothing me like that. I've been married to you for a long time, Lash. Don't even think of pretending something isn't up. I can tell." She put the basket down, and moved toward him, cupping his face. "Tell me."

He didn't say anything. Instead, he pulled out a piece of paper, and handed it to her. Frowning, she took the paper and read it.

"A vasectomy. This appointment is for Friday, Lash."

"I know."

"Is there something wrong? Are you ill?"

"No, I'm not ill."

"Why would the doctor recommend this?" Angel asked.

"He didn't recommend it. I asked for it."

"You did? Why would you do that?" She held the piece of paper, but she couldn't believe it. Lash wanted a vasectomy, and he wanted it willingly.

"So we don't have to have any more children."

She gasped, stepping away from him. "You don't want any more children?"

"No, I don't. After everything we've been through, I'm making the right choice."

Angel stared at her husband, then down at the paper. "You weren't going to tell me."

"No, I wasn't. I was just going to get the procedure done, but I couldn't. I had to tell you."

"And when I wanted more kids, what then?"

"We'd try, and when nothing happened, you'd move on."

Tears filled her eyes, and slipped down her cheeks. "After everything we've been through, you were going to be this deceitful to me."

"I'm doing it for your own protection."

"What for? What do I need protecting from?" she asked.

"Look at our track record when it comes to

having kids. We're not exactly up there as great candidates for pregnancy," he said. "You lost one—"

"Through the enemy of the club!"

"Anthony was a hard pregnancy."

"He was my first one to come to term. All firstborn babies are difficult." She couldn't believe what she was hearing.

"Then Chloe."

"Another attack, Lash. None of these incidents are anything out of the ordinary. Not with giving birth to Anthony. He was my first baby. Chloe was a lot easier. The factors surrounding us were what changed everything. No woman should have to face death, but I signed on for that when I fell in love with you."

"And I can't risk losing you. Pregnancy is too big of a risk. I'm going to get this procedure."

Angel gasped as tears fell from her eyes. Spinning on her heel, she made her way toward the door, then stopped. "I've felt a lot of pain in my life. I've been hurt, I've tried to kill myself, I've been shot, and throughout all of that, I've never felt pain like the words you've just delivered has given to me."

"Angel?"

"No, don't. I love you, Lash. Flaws and all. That love will never stop. If you go and have that procedure, don't come back home."

"Baby—"

"It'll be over. You made that decision without asking me. You made that decision on your own, and if you do this alone you will stay. I can't be with someone who'll deceive me."

With that, she left, turning on her heel, and going to the one room that always gave her comfort, to her children's rooms. First she went to Chloe's room, staring down at her darling girl. She vowed to protect her babies, to protect the club. How could Lash do that to her? She regretted her words the moment she said them. There was no way she could leave Lash. He was her life. He filled her heart with so much love that at times she thought she would burst with happiness. No matter how much she wanted to run to him now, she couldn't. He'd hurt her.

Next, she went to Anthony's room, and chuckled. He was sitting reading. "I thought I put you to bed."

"I wasn't tired, and I like reading."

"Did you hear?" she asked.

"You and Dad fighting?" She nodded. "A little bit."

"I'm sorry."

"Why? Tab says Tiny and Eva fight a lot, too. So does Tate and Murphy. Fighting is normal."

"It's not."

He frowned. "Doesn't it mean you love each other?"

"I don't know, sweetie."

"You're fighting because you're angry, and you're hurt. If you feel those things, then it must mean you love each other, and I know you and Dad love each other. A lot."

"We do."

Anthony smiled. "Would you like me to read to you?"

"Yes, that would be lovely."

Chapter Eleven

One day later

Millie hummed to herself as she walked down the street. She was walking down the same street she'd walked thousands of times only today was different. She was walking down the street with a sore pussy, and bruises on her hips. There was no way to wipe the smile from her face. She was so damn happy, and walking on cloud nine. They had made love three more times, and she felt different.

Everything seemed brighter, happier, more alive than ever before.

Entering the café, she spotted the Skulls women in the corner, talking. It was Friday lunch time, and she'd closed the shop to have lunch with them, only for a break. She had to go to the post office to make some deliveries, and now was as good a time as any.

Lacey spotted her first, giving a whistle. "Is it me, or do I detect something different about you?"

Millie chuckled, removing her jacket, and taking a seat. "I had a wonderful night."

"So you and Baker, you're together-together?" Tate asked.

"Yep. We're officially together." She tucked some of her hair behind her ear, and turned toward the barrister.

"I've got your order, ladies. I'll be right over."

"Thank you."

Turning back, she saw how sad Angel looked as she kept gazing at the clock.

"Are you okay?" Millie asked.

Angel was usually the happiest, constantly bouncing around without a care in the world.

"I'm sorry. I'm not the best company right now. I'm kind of in a crisis."

"What kind?" Tate asked.

"The kind that could depend on divorce or not."

Every single Skull woman turned toward her.

"Divorce?" Sophia, Kelsey, Eva, and Sunshine asked.

"Yeah, divorce. It seems like Lash wants to take our childbearing matters into his own hands, and with it, he was willing to be deceitful. I said some really bad things, and now I'm scared. What if he wants to divorce me? Oh, God, I'm so scared. I love Lash."

"I don't have a clue what is going on," Emily said. She was Blaine's old lady, and the mother of Darcy.

"Lash is scheduled to have a vasectomy today, only I would like us to have more kids. He doesn't want to take the risk. Instead of telling me about it, he tried to hide it, and with it, I don't know, I just felt betrayed. Even though he told me in the end. God, I love him. I love him so much." She leaned forward, pressing her face into her hands. "I can't stand this. My stomach is twisting and turning. I can't. I just, I love Lash so much, but how can he think to hurt me like that? And what if he leaves me?"

"I don't think he tried to hurt you," Prue said.

"No?"

"What I've noticed with Lash is when it comes to you, the guy can't think straight. You're all he wants, all he'll ever want. The thought of losing you, it's too much for him to deal with." Prue was closest to Angel, and placed her hand on her back, rubbing it, trying to give her comfort.

"I don't know what to do. I told him if he went to that damn appointment, and went through with it, we were done." Angel pressed her face back into her hand.

"I'm a horrible person."

"You're nowhere near horrible," Tate said. "Believe me, I know."

"Don't we all," Prue said.

"Don't start. You're as bad as me."

"Not on your life," Prue said.

"Ladies, we're here for Angel right now. You can bicker another time, and make it all about you," Eva said.

"I feel sick," Angel said.

"Do you really think I'd pick a stupid operation over you?" Lash said, startling them all.

Angel looked up, and there Lash stood, behind Millie.

"You didn't go?" she asked.

"Of course I didn't go. I was doing what I thought was right for you, for us, not to get a divorce out of it." He moved toward Angel, kneeling down in front of her. "When are you going to realize that you mean more to me than anything else? I will move heaven and earth to make you happy."

"I'm being selfish," she said. "I shouldn't have said that to you, and I regretted it the moment I said it. I was just so hurt. I love you so much."

"It has taken you a long time to stand up for yourself, and you were right. This wasn't a decision that only I should have taken."

"I love you, Lash."

"I love you, too."

Millie watched as the two kissed, passionately. She thought about Baker. It was hard not to think about him.

"I'm going to head to the clubhouse. I've got some business to take care of. I'll see you tonight for dinner." He kissed Angel, and then he left.

"Wow, now that is so romantic," Rose said. "You

two are like serious movie couple material."

Angel blushed. "Stop."

"I'm being serious," Rose said. "Hardy's like the worst hero ever. He cheated on me."

"And you took him back, you live happily ever after, and he's the bad boy turned good," Tate said. "That doesn't count. Angel and Lash are the ultimate."

"I think we're all straying off track right now. Let's remember, Millie lost that V-card."

Millie chuckled. "There's nothing to say."

"Was he lame in the bedroom?" Tate asked.

"No, not at all." Millie stared down at her hands as she remembered the feel of Baker inside her. "It was the best night of my life." There had been some pain but not a whole lot. She loved it, and had wanted to do it again. Baker had left her this morning with the promise to speed up the process of buying his apartment. He wanted them to move in together. "Baker is a real gentleman."

"Don't forget. Men want a lady in the kitchen, and a whore in the bedroom," Tate said.

"Everyone knows that," Lacey said. "You're not going to say anything else?"

Millie shook her head. "I'm afraid not." Last night was going to remain with her, and she had no intention of sharing that with anyone.

The rest of the lunch went by without much event. Angel perked up, and by the end of everything, Prue and Tate were at each other's throats. It was kind of funny to watch. Millie didn't know who won or not.

Angel invited her to dinner that Sunday with her and Lash, which she accepted. Millie thought dinner would have been at the club but Angel told her not. She didn't always cook at the club.

Heading back to her shop, Millie opened it back

up, and was humming to herself as she put some of the toys right on the shelf. Minutes passed, and the door opened, letting her know a new customer had arrived. She turned around with a smile on her face, and froze.

"Hello, sister," Bethany said.

Bethany, her sister, the woman who liked to make sure her life was miserable stood in the doorway. "Wow, you really didn't grow up, did you?"

"What are you doing here?" Millie asked, feeling every part of herself start to shrivel up a little.

"Is that any way to talk to your sister?"

"I've been here a long time, and you've never found the need to come and visit me." There was no love inside Millie when she looked at Bethany. That had died a long time ago. Her sister went out of her way to make her life a misery.

"Let's just say I bumped into someone, and he had some fun things to say about you."

"Brian?"

"Yeah, Brian, remember him?" Bethany asked. "I sure do. He's a tasty little morsel who I can pick right off the shelf."

"Yeah, I remember you screwing him on my wedding day."

"Sweetie, I was fucking him a hell of a lot longer than that. He was really good in the sack as well. I mean, really good. I've never had one better so far. Then again, I've never had an MC member either. You're always the good girl, Millie. I only need to be the good girl when it matters."

"You mean when you're trying to turn Grandma against me? Cut me out of the will?"

"What?" Millie was confused.

"Have you spoken to Grandma lately?" Bethany asked.

Millie frowned. "It has been a couple of months. She's been busy, why?"

"So no conversations about what she's doing?"

"I'm not about to talk to you about Grandma, Bethany. Whatever she decides to do, it's up to her."

"It's not like you deserve anything. Look at you, do you really think you'll keep an MC guy for long? No one likes a fat ass."

Millie stared at her, waiting.

"What? You're not going to tell me I can't have him?" Bethany asked. "You already know you're going to lose. Who'd want you, over me?"

"I'd take Millie any day," Baker said, startling both women.

Millie turned toward the door to see Baker glaring at Bethany.

"I take it this is the sister?"

"So she's been spreading rumors about me that are completely unfounded."

"Is that what you do to make everyone think you're a fucking princess? Blame your sister? I heard everything. You're a fucking bitch."

Bethany smiled, and Millie winced as her sister swung her hips from side to side, moving up to him.

"What's the matter? Are you jealous? Baby, I've got skills that will make your mind pop. Leave my frumpy little bitch of a sister behind. I can show you what a real woman is made of." Bethany went to stroke his face, and Baker looked utterly disgusted.

"Don't even think of touching me. I've got a woman, and she's all I need." Baker released her, moving behind Millie, and banding an arm around her. "I was hoping to catch you alone."

"I'm sorry."

"Is that how it's going to be? Oh well, you'll soon

SAM CRESCENT

see there's no getting rid of me. I've had every other boyfriend you've wanted, Millie. I'll have him, too."

Millie frowned. "There's only ever been Brian."

"Oh, didn't you know? You used to have some boys come to call. I showed them the error of their ways. No one wants a fatty. Bye for now." Bethany left the shop. Millie's nerves were totally shot.

"There's my sister. Most men fall at her feet."

"I'm not most men, and there's no way in hell I'd ever pick her over you. She's a fucking viper."

"I know. It's a shame no one else has ever seen the real her." She pushed some of her hair off her face, and turned to smile at him. "Hello, handsome."

Baker slammed his lips down on hers, making her moan. Banding her hands around his neck, she gasped as he gripped her ass, tugging her close.

"I want to fuck you so damn bad."

"I want that, too."

He pulled away. "You do?"

"Yeah, I do. I want it more than anything."

She went in for another kiss, only he moved away, going toward the door to flick the lock in place. Seconds later he was pulling her toward her office.

"Strip," he said.

"What?"

"I want you completely naked, now."

He went for his belt and started to unbuckle it. Biting her lip, Millie didn't argue, and got to opening up her jeans. Sliding them down her thighs, she tore off her shirt. The moment she was completely naked, Baker was on her. He lifted her up, pressing her down on the desk. Papers flew in all directions.

"This isn't going to take long." He tore into a condom, rolling the latex down over his length. Aligning the tip to her core, he slammed all the way inside,

161

making her cry out. "You're so fucking tight."

She stared down at where they were joined, his cock slick with her cream even with the condom protecting them.

He pulled out of her until only the tip remained before fucking her hard, repeatedly pounding inside her.

"You like this, baby. You like me owning your pussy?"

"Yes, yes, I love it."

She loved it when he talked dirty, when he got her all wet and ready for him.

"No one else will ever drive me wild. My dick, Millie, it belongs to you."

"Please, I need to come."

Baker took her hand, placing it between her thighs. "Make yourself come."

She stroked over her clit as he pounded inside her, the force of his thrusts heightening her need. With a few strokes, she came, screaming his name.

He grunted out, slamming all the way inside her, and groaning. His cock pulsed sending more pleasure shooting through her entire body.

Both of them were panting, and Baker groaned. She saw him check the time, and drop his head to her breasts. "Babe, that took us ten minutes."

"Oh. Is that not good?"

"I was hoping to last a little longer, but when I get you naked, I lose all thought process."

"I'm not going to complain about that." She cupped his cheek. "Thank you so much for stopping by."

"Your sister, she gets a great deal of pleasure out of hurting you."

"It doesn't matter."

"It does to me. I'm not going to let her hurt you. Not now, not ever."

"There's not a lot we can do about it. Maybe if she's ignored, she'll leave," Millie said, only hoping her sister would.

"Do you believe that?"

"It's what I hope."

****

Bethany didn't leave. No, she attempted to visit the club, several times. Baker often found her trying to lure in several of the club members, even some of the Prospects. None of the men wanted her. Besides the fact nearly all of them were happily married, the other members saw her viciousness. The Skulls was no longer a club intent on getting into any drama. The past ten years had been filled with enough drama and heartache to last everyone a lifetime. Bethany smelled of trouble, and they were all keeping a wide berth. Also, she kept asking about Grandma, which annoyed her. Bethany never cared about their Grandma before.

A couple of days before the Halloween party, Baker sat at the dining table of the clubhouse, drinking a cup of coffee. The club was heavily made up with white cobweb streamers, pumpkins, candy, and moving objects that went off if you moved past them.

Angel entered after dropping the kids off.

"I thought you were going to get your hair done?" Baker asked.

"I was. Millie's sister was there, and it looked like Lacey was about to pierce her throat with a pair of scissors. I can't believe Millie and Bethany are related. They're two completely different people."

"Complete opposites."

"I know it's strange for me to say, but I really don't like that woman."

"You don't like someone?" Lash asked. "Usually, baby, you're the one who tries to find a redeeming quality in everyone."

"I know. It's kind of hard to do when the woman in question seems to get some sick twisted joy out of hurting her sister. She likes to talk about how she had sex with Millie's ex." Angel shook her head. "It's just wrong."

"Sister has a pretty violent past as well," Whizz said. "I've told Lacey to ignore her. My woman has more chance of going to jail than getting away with Bethany's murder."

"None of the women like her. I for one can't stand her," Sophia said, entering the room. "I've been to see Millie as well. It's just making Millie withdraw more into herself."

"She's seen this type of shit before. I spoke to her about it. Her sister tends to worm her way between Millie and her friends, spread vile gossip, leaving Millie alone," Baker said.

Eva snorted. "Not going to happen. Not with this club. She's probably pissed she hasn't been able to screw you yet." She pointed at Baker.

"Not happening. My heart is with Millie. Always will be."

"Any chance that heart of yours is leaning towards marriage?" Whizz asked.

"Not yet, no. You and Lacey shouldn't bet on people's feelings, or their future."

Whizz shrugged. "It keeps our love interesting, and it stops us from becoming bored."

"Some of us are lucky enough that we'll never get bored," Lash said, taking Angel's hand, and kissing it.

"I wish there was something we could do," Angel said.

"Be there for her. She's used to no one wanting anything to do with her. The only woman who ever showed her any love and affection lives in Italy. Her grandma." Baker ran some fingers through her hair. "I'm going to head out to see her. Have some lunch. Make sure she's still coming to the party."

He said his goodbyes and made his way toward his bike.

"Ah, just the biker I wanted to see," Bethany said.

Baker turned toward her and shook his head. "Not going to happen. Not in this lifetime."

"It's only a matter of time before you cave. I'll give you props. You're a lot stronger than her last boyfriend. Brian didn't put up a fight. I was dancing on his dick before the end of the day."

"Go home." He straddled his bike, ignoring anymore of her words. Baker had come to the conclusion that ignoring her was the best way to get rid of her.

He rode toward Millie's shop. His woman was putting her sign out, and he saw the sadness in her eyes. Her shoulders were slumped, and her eyes looked like she'd been crying.

Parking the bike, he moved toward her.

"Baker, I didn't expect you," she said, pushing a stray strand of hair off her face.

He pulled her into his arms, kissing the top of her head. "I'll always come for you. I missed you last night. What's wrong?"

"I was tired. I didn't feel too good."

Tilting her head back, he stared into her eyes. "Don't let her hurt you," he said.

"It's easy to say that. I don't know. I feel like the last nine years have all been a waste." Tears filled her eyes, and started to fall. "Fort Wills was supposed to be my start, my chance to just be myself. Not stupid fat Millie who can't do anything right, not even keep a boyfriend!"

"Hey. You're the most beautiful woman I've ever met, and you've got a boyfriend standing right here, right now, and I promise you, I'll not stray. I'm like a loyal dog. You've already taken me, now you've got no chance of ever getting rid of me."

She took a deep breath. "I'm sorry."

"Don't worry about it."

They made their way inside her shop, and he noticed one display of small toys had been toppled over. "Bethany?"

"Yeah, she came in this morning, and said a few horrible things. It's just like being at home, only worse."

He kissed her temple. "Don't worry, everything will be okay. I promise."

Baker helped her pick up the mess that Bethany had made, and stayed with her 'til lunchtime. He ate lunch with her, and asked about the Halloween party. She was still going with him, but she was also a little scared because Bethany would find some way to ruin it. He couldn't stay with her after lunch as he had some business still to attend to. After he took her back to her shop, Baker had to leave.

Leaving her was the hardest thing he'd ever had to do, and wondered if there was any way to get rid of Bethany, he'd do it.

****

Millie was finishing up her packaging of recent internet orders when Bethany returned. She'd called her grandma asking if something had gone wrong, and there hadn't been anything. Her grandmother had told her that she'd made some decisions, and that Millie wasn't to worry. When Millie asked about Bethany's reappearance, her grandmother had said to get rid of Bethany, that she wasn't happy with certain changes being made. For some reason her grandmother was being really vague. It wasn't

Millie's place to ask about the will, and whatever she decided, she trusted her grandmother. This was not a social call from Bethany, and it was simply a visit to make her life miserable because Grandma had always preferred her over Bethany. Grandma had told her to be careful and to watch her back.

"Well, I have to say my visit has been really disappointing," Bethany said.

"I haven't seen you in nine years. What could you possibly want?"

"Let's just say our dad has told me something, and I don't like it. Grandma thinks she can get away with changing this family, and she's wrong. You're scum, exactly like her. You don't deserve the Levy name, nor any of the perks. It's just so easy to take from you, Millie. You never put up a fight, and you always look so miserable. Also, you're fat, and I really don't like fat people. You're gross, disgusting, and to be quite frank, it's humiliating sharing the same name as you. You're not even fit to be a Levy. Grandma won't get away with what she's done. We're going to make sure she pays."

Millie stared at her sister, and thought about what Whizz said.

"Then leave. I don't see why you're even here." It was time to finally let go of whatever crap her sister wanted to do, or wished to do. "Actually, we've been over this. I know why you're here. Scrap my last question. Fine, try and steal Baker away from me. Try and get all of The Skulls to turn their backs on me. Go ahead, I dare you, because I'm done with you. I'm bored, and I'm not going to allow you to control any other part of my life. You mean nothing to me, now and for the rest of my life. I don't give a fuck about the Levy name. You know why? It's embarrassing. People hear it, and think of you, Mom, and Dad, and they're disgusted by you, just like me."

Bethany looked totally shocked.

"I suggest you leave before I call the cops."

Millie stared at her sister, and any kind of need or wish to be friends with her died. Over the years Bethany had destroyed any kind of love that she may have had for the other woman. Going to the phone, she lifted it up, intent on taking matters in her own hands.

"We'll see who gets the last laugh!" Bethany left, and with it Millie could take a deep breath.

She was done with being bullied, she was done with being made a laughingstock, and she was done with a sister filled with hate.

Chapter Twelve

Baker flipped Millie over onto her stomach, kissing from her neck down her spine. "You turn me on when you tell me shit like this," he said.

"What? How I finally told my sister to fuck off, and how much I enjoyed actually doing it?" she asked.

"Yeah, for having trust in me, and in the club."

"I just wish I'd told her to go and fuck herself a long time ago."

He kissed her neck, biting down on her pulse. "You said the word fuck, you naughty girl."

He nibbled on her neck, sucking on her pulse.

"You're turning me bad with that wicked tongue of yours."

"It always feels so good to be bad." He kissed down her back, going to her ass. Drawing her knees up, he slid a finger deep inside her pussy, thrusting in deep. His apartment should be ready in a couple of days, and he'd forced Millie to come to the clubhouse. He didn't want her to be home, and he wanted her to be surrounded by the club. The Skulls loved her, and no one was going to let Bethany hurt her. "I've been asked when we're going to get married."

He slid a third finger inside her, teasing her clit with his thumb.

She groaned, and thrust against him. "I thought we agreed no marriage in Vegas right now."

"What if we let Whizz win?"

"You want to get married? Is this a proposal, Baker?"

He moved his hand away from her pussy, and slammed his cock deep inside her. Lifting her up so that her back was flush against him, he cupped her tits, teasing the peaks with his cum soaked fingers. He'd lick them clean later. First he intended to fuck her pussy raw so she couldn't remember her own name.

"I'm thinking it's what we should do." Holding her tight against him, Baker growled. "I can't hold back any longer." Right there, pounding his cock inside her pussy, he spilled his heart out. "I love you, Millie. I love you so damn much that I can't even think straight. I want us to be together, to have a family."

She turned her head. "You can't do this, not right now."

He moved his hand down to stroke her clit, and riding her pussy hard, he brought her to orgasm, relishing the screams echoing off the walls. The rooms were as soundproof as the club could get them.

"That's it, come for me, baby. Come all over my cock." Pushing her down onto the bed, he grabbed her hips, and pounded inside her, thrusting as deep as he could go. Staring in the mirror across from his room, he admired the image of them together. It was perfect, pure, and his heart soared higher. Millie was all his, and he belonged to her.

Thrusting inside her one final time, he released into the condom, holding onto his woman as he did. Kissing her neck, he collapsed to the bed, pulling her in his arms.

"Baker," she said.

"Yeah, baby."

"I love you, too." She looked up at him, her hand placed over his heart. "I'll marry you whenever you want."

"Christmas always seems to work."

"Then Christmas it will be." She moved up, kissing his lips, and then straddled his waist.

He groaned. "You're fucking insatiable. I

awakened a monster."

"I've been asleep for twenty-nine years, so it's time for me to catch up on all that I'd missed." She leaned forward about to kiss him when sudden banging happened on the door.

"I'm coming in," Whizz said.

"Fuck off!" Baker yelled. Millie screamed, darting off the bed, and hiding as Whizz opened the door. "What the fuck! Get out."

"You've both got to get dressed. Millie, your shop is on fire."

"What?"

"We've got to go, now."

Baker shoved Whizz out of the door, and while Millie was getting changed, he tugged some clothes on. "Whatever happens, the club is with you."

The next half an hour was a blur as Baker rode with Millie on the back of his bike in time to see the entire shop go up in flames.

Millie jumped off the bike and stared at the mess. Firefighters were trying to stop the flames, but it was too late. Toys, bears, extremely flammable materials were inside, and Baker held her, pulling her away from the heat.

"Bethany did this," she said.

He didn't doubt it. Holding onto his woman, he felt the club at his back, watching, waiting, planning.

"Everything is gone," she said.

"You've got me, and we'll get through this."

He held her tightly, offering her as much comfort as possible. At the end of the evening, after he put her to bed, he made his way down to the rest of the club.

All of them were waiting.

"It was Bethany," Whizz said. "I put security cameras all around Millie's store when Andrew was on the attack. I never removed them. I thought it would be good for us to keep an eye on her. I'm glad I trusted my instincts."

"You've got proof?" Angel asked.

"Yes."

"Then I think it's time for me and the girls to pay Bethany a visit." Angel turned to Lash. "Do you still have your informant at the police?" she asked.

"Yeah, it's a new guy. The name's Lawrence Arnold."

"The new sheriff?" Tiny asked.

"Yeah, he wanted to be on good terms. He likes Fort Wills, and the town likes us. I can arrange for you to have time with Bethany, and for Lawrence to hold back. He owes me a favor," Lash said.

"Then do it."

"Are you sure about that?" Baker asked.

"If our kids can look after each other, then I think it's only fair that the women take care of this. Millie is one of us. She's your old lady, and right now, she's under threat. I don't like it. We won't hurt Bethany, but we'll let her know who she's dealing with."

Lash whistled. "Saucy."

"You stay here with Millie," Angel said. "She needs you right now."

"We'll all help with the shop," Tiny said. "She's one of us. She's your old lady."

Tears filled Baker's eyes, and he looked away. "Thank you."

"We're a family, Baker. It's what we do." Angel moved toward him, patting his chest. "Go and keep an eye on her."

He left the others, knowing he was safe to comfort his woman when she needed him most. Entering the room, he saw she was wide awake, staring at the wall. Removing his clothes, he climbed in beside her, kissing her shoulder.

"She hates me so much that she couldn't help herself, and she tore apart something I love."

"The club is going to take care of her, Millie. We've got the recording, and Bethany isn't going to get away with it."

"She'll find some way out of it."

"Not this time." He captured her cheek, and turned her head to look at him. "The club is going to handle it."

"Why would they?"

"Because you belong to me. You're my woman, Millie, and when you become a Skull old lady, you become part of the club. We all love you, and we're all going to take care of you."

Tears spilled out of the corners of her eyes as she wrapped her arms around him. "I love you so much as well. I've been waiting my whole life for someone to love me for me."

"We do. We love you, forever, and for always."

He held her tightly as tears fell from her eyes. It was a vow he'd made to himself before coming home. If he wasn't ready to love Millie with all of his heart, he wasn't coming back.

She owned his heart and soul, and there was no way he was ever going to fight her for them back.

Millie was his number one.

****

Prue kicked open the door to Bethany's apartment. When the woman made a mad dash for it, Lacey was in, grabbing the woman by her hair, and throwing her against the wall. Tate followed, wrapping her fingers around the woman's neck.

"This is assault."

"What do you have to say about arson?" Angel asked.

The color in Bethany's face disappeared. "I don't have a clue what you're talking about."

"You spent so long hating your sister, you didn't even care that someone could be watching. Your hatred, your greed has gotten the better of you."

"No one was with me. I made sure of it."

Angel walked toward the television and DVD player. Sliding in the disk, she pressed for it to play, and turned to watch. With every second that passed, she saw Bethany look less triumphant and more scared.

The footage showed clearly what Bethany was doing. Breaking into Millie's shop, trashing it, and the footage inside did the rest. She threw petrol over the teddy bears, costumes, and other toys, then lit the match, tossing it inside. Bethany left, but she watched for ten minutes as the entire building went up in flames.

Bethany tried to fight the hold on her neck. Tate squeezed, slamming her back against the wall.

"What is it to you bitches? She's a fucking fat whore, and she's not worth your time. She stole everything from me. My inheritance, everything. You think I don't know about that! Dad called me up earlier, and told me everything is going to her. It's mine. I'm the oldest. It's all supposed to be mine. Not hers. Grandma is selling the fucking company, and tossing us aside. That's not right. They're fucking disgusting."

"She's a Skull woman. She belongs to us, and you never try to hurt someone I love." Angel stepped forward, moving right up into Bethany's face. She couldn't believe Millie had been hurt so much in the past by someone this vile. She would make sure her friend was never going to be hurt again.

"Why did you wait?" Lacey asked. "Why wait

nine years to come and hurt her?"

"You think I cared about that bitch? She was gone, and I didn't have to look at her. When Brian told me he saw her, I couldn't resist coming and ruining her. Then Dad told me what was happening, and that I couldn't let stand."

"You're fucking deranged," Tate said.

"Whatever. Is this where you expect me to demand a deal? Fine, how much do you want? We're fighting the sale, and that bitch of a Grandma better watch her back. Now, how much do you want?" Bethany asked.

"No, we don't want anything. I just wanted you to know that you messed with Millie, and you messed with all of us. We are a family. You start on one, you start on the other." Angel made her way toward the door. "She's in here."

Tate released her, and Bethany gasped as the sheriff entered. "Bethany Levy, you are under arrest."

He told her the crime, and started to read her her rights.

"No, you can't do this. It's not supposed to happen. No, you bitch, you fucking bitch."

Angel watched as Lawrence dragged a screaming Bethany out of the hotel.

"You should have slapped her," Eva said.

"There was no need. She got the message loud and clear," Angel said. Staring at the blazing fire on the screen, Angel hated seeing violence, and this was just the worst kind. "Let's go home."

****

In the weeks after Millie's house and shop were burned down, Bethany had no choice but to admit to the charges as there was no doubt of who it was. Millie stayed at the club, and when she could, visited the wreckage, but there was nothing she could do. The damage to the building was too dangerous, and nothing could be salvaged.

The best course of action was in time to completely demolish, and start from the beginning. In the meantime, she still went to the Halloween party with Baker, dressed as a dead nurse, while Baker dressed as a zombie patient.

His apartment became available for the two of them, so Millie moved in with him. She spent most of her time following him around, watching what he did with his time, and for the club. When she could no longer stand riding around, and not doing something, she took a job in Lacey's beauty shop. She mopped floors, dealt with appointments, and tried to make herself busy.

Her life may have been hectic with her shop, but her life with Baker, that was the best part. Moving in with him had only cemented their relationship, and she didn't regret it. She loved watching Baker sleep. Especially in the early hours of the morning just before his alarm went off. He always looked so at peace, and then when the alarm went off, he'd moan, slam his hand down on the offending sound, and smile at her as if she was the most beautiful woman in the world. He'd make love to her, awakening her body for the day.

After breakfast together, he'd drop her off at the beauty shop, and then see her for lunch. She'd work the rest of the afternoon and drive herself home, waiting for Baker to come home. Dinner was a passionate affair, which usually ended with them both being naked.

Sex played a big part of their life.

So did conversation.

So did love.

They had it all, and Millie knew she was doing the right thing as she sat at the table waiting for him to come home. She stared down at the velvet box, wondering what Baker would think of her proposal. She was completely naked, and hoped it would help for him to accept her question. Baker was always using sex to get her to agree to everything.

"Hey, baby, I'm home," Baker said. "I've been having to do Christmas shopping for the club. We needed a new tree, and new de—" He stopped the moment he saw her.

"Hello, Baker," she said, pushing some hair off her shoulder. "Take a seat."

"What's going on?" he asked.

"Nothing."

"Babe, you've never been naked for me to come home to before."

She chuckled. "That's okay. Are you distracted?"

"A lot."

"Good." She put the velvet box on the table top.

"What is this?"

"Open it, go on."

He took the box, and opened it.

"Baker, Jaxson Jones, will you marry me?" she asked.

"Holy shit."

"I love you, and there's no one else I'd ever want."

Baker looked at the ring she'd given to him. "This is real, isn't it?"

"Yes." Her heart was pounding, and she didn't know what to do if he told her no.

"You got to this first." Baker grabbed a box out of his pocket. "I was going to ask you the exact same thing."

Millie opened the box, and tears filled her eyes.

"You know Lacey is going to fire you?" Baker

asked.

"Does that mean you'll marry me?"

"Yes, will you marry me?"

"Of course."

They both opened the boxes, and slid the rings onto each other's fingers. Baker grabbed her ass, pulling her close to him. "Come on, I want us to celebrate."

"Baker?"

"Yeah."

"I was thinking we could go to Vegas," she said. "I've got the tickets right here." She grabbed the plane tickets that she'd bought. "Do you have plans this Friday?"

"Yes, this Friday, I'm going to be getting married."

"I love you, Baker."

"Babe, you've given me my life back, and there's no place I'd want to be than with you." He picked her up and carried her through to their bedroom.

Millie held onto him, even as he began to make love to her. It didn't take long before the headboard started to slam against the wall.

This was the love of her life, and she was never going to let him go. Millie wanted to spend the rest of her life showing him how much she loved him.

"I love you, Millie," he said, later that night. "You won't regret picking me for everything."

She cupped his cheek. "You picked me as well." Leaning up, she pressed her lips against his. "Let's make the next fifty years perfect."

"I'm always up for the challenge."

****

Sally wrapped the jacket around her body as she stared up at the stars. Her love of the sky had never once diminished. Her love of school had certain started to go.

She didn't love it as much as she used to, and college was by far the worst decision she'd ever made.

"I thought I'd find you out here," Steven said.

She turned to find the object of another worry walking toward her. Steven. The love she'd thought would never be. He stood in front of her, looking a little confused. She'd gone back to college with the promise that she'd talk to him soon.

"You've been avoiding me," he said.

"I know."

"Why?"

She looked back up at the stars. "I don't know. It seemed easier somehow."

He moved up behind her. "I'm not going anywhere. I'll wait for you for the rest of my life." He wrapped his arms around her.

"What are my mom and dad going to say?" Sally asked. "There's no way this is going to work."

"We can make it work. I'll do anything to make this work, Sally." He tilted her head back, running his thumb across her lip. "You've just got to have a little faith in me."

She stared into his eyes, and wondered what she should do. Whizz would hurt him if he knew the truth. Lacey would be worried if she told her.

Her leg made them both even more protective.

"Do you have enough trust in me to take a chance?"

Did she?

Sally looked at the stars, wishing she knew what the future could bring.

"Sally, are you ready to head back?" Drew said, calling toward her.

Steven growled, and she tensed up.

One day soon she'd have to make a choice, and

she only hoped she made the right one.

Epilogue

A couple of months later

"Grandma, this is my husband, Baker," Millie said.

Baker stared at the older woman, wondering if she'd be happy with him marrying her granddaughter.

"Husband?"

"Yeah, I told you that I'd gotten married, remember?"

Her grandmother glared. "I remember everything." The older woman stood. "Are you not going to give me a hug? It has been too long since you were last here, and I heard what Bethany did to you. Stupid girl, I'm so sorry I couldn't come back home."

Millie hugged her grandmother. "It's fine. I'm happy. Bethany is paying for what she did, and I'm not going to regret what happened. It brought me closer to Baker."

"She moved in with me," Baker said.

Her grandmother looked at him. "I should have warned you about my plans, sweetie. I'm sorry your shop had to pay."

"It's fine. You did what you had to."

"I can't believe I created a boy so greedy that he had someone like Bethany."

Millie loved her grandmother so much. "Don't blame yourself.

Grandmother sniffled and turned to Baker. "So you're the man that not only fell in love with my granddaughter, but then married her in some cheap Vegas church."

"Grandma!"

"I love Millie, Mrs. Levy, and I couldn't wait in

case someone stole her away from me. She has been hurt a lot in the past, and I've been the cause of some of that pain. I wasn't going to add to it. She owns my heart." He wrapped his arm around Millie's waist, kissing her lips. "I hope you can forgive us. We'd waited long enough, and we didn't want to wait another moment."

Grandma Levy stared, and then broke into a grin. "It's about time you opened your eyes, Millie. This man is so damn handsome." She gripped Baker's cheeks. "Cute. Come on, it's time for some food."

"You're happy?" Millie asked.

"Sweetie, it wasn't about what I wanted. It was only about what you wanted. Does he make you happy?"

"Yes. Yes, he does."

"Then nothing else matters. I will go and do us all some food. I may be old, but I'm not dead yet. Sit, enjoy the sun, and be ready for me to give you the third degree."

Baker watched as the older woman made her way inside the house.

"Do you think she approves?" he asked.

"Yes. Grandma doesn't cook for just anyone. What about you, are you still happy for me to be your wife?"

"Get me alone in a room with you, and I'll show you how damn happy I am to be married to you."

She giggled, and he sank his fingers into her hair. They had been married before Christmas at a Vegas church, and then had a huge celebration at the clubhouse. "You're my old lady," he said.

"And you're my old man."

Wrapping her arms around his neck, Millie smiled up at him, and with every other time, he fell a little harder for her.

He knew the next fifty years were not going to be

enough, but it was a start.

When it came to love, there was never enough time, and with Millie, she was his number one, and he was going to show her for the rest of his life.

The End

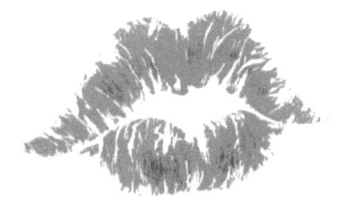

EVERNIGHT PUBLISHING ®

www.evernightpublishing.com